The toddler had Lily's eyes. And his hair and dimple.

Justin dragged his gaze from the little girl and met Lily's. Emotions chased across her expressive features—surprise replaced by swift guilt that was quickly banished by the defiant lift of her chin.

Then she slammed the door shut.

Shock held Justin paralyzed for one stunned moment before he pounded on the door panels. "Lily!"

The door flew open.

"What do you want? What are you doing here?" she demanded.

"I'm in town. I wanted to say hello." He couldn't take his eyes off the little girl. "What's her name?"

"Ava." Lily gathered the toddler closer, her stance protective. "You've said hello, now I want you to leave."

"Not until you tell me about Ava. She's mine, isn't she?"

Dear Reader,

I was delighted when I was asked to join three close friends in writing THE HUNT FOR CINDERELLA miniseries—the four of us had a wonderful time brainstorming ideas for our connected books. I fell in love with all of the brothers but especially with the youngest, Justin, and writing his story gave me a chance to combine my favorite kind of hero—a cowboy—with a heroine from the big city.

The stories are set in Seattle, Washington, one of my favorite cities. Who can resist the fabulous coffee shops or the exotic Pike Place Market? One sunny weekend I caught a cross-Sound ferry to the Seattle suburb of Ballard, where my daughter and I browsed the shops along Ballard Avenue. I knew instantly it was the perfect neighborhood for my heroine's Princess Lily Boutique.

I hope you'll enjoy reading *The Princess and the Cowboy* as much as I loved writing it. And come back to the Pacific Northwest next month, in *The Millionaire and the Glass Slipper* by Christine Flynn, to follow another Hunt brother hunting for his Cinderella!

Warmly,

Lois Faye Dyer
www.LoisFayeDyer.com

THE PRINCESS
AND THE COWBOY

LOIS FAYE DYER

Silhouette®

SPECIAL EDITION®

Published by Silhouette Books

America's Publisher of Contemporary Romance

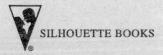

SILHOUETTE BOOKS

ISBN-13: 978-0-373-24865-0
ISBN-10:   0-373-24865-2

THE PRINCESS AND THE COWBOY

Visit Silhouette Books at www.eHarlequin.com

Printed in U.S.A.

Books by Lois Faye Dyer

Silhouette Special Edition

Lonesome Cowboy #1038
He's Got His Daddy's Eyes #1129
The Cowboy Takes a Wife #1198
The Only Cowboy for Caitlin #1253
Cattleman's Courtship #1306
Cattleman's Bride-to-Be #1457
Practice Makes Pregnant #1569
Cattleman's Heart #1611
†*The Prince's Bride* #1640
*Luke's Proposal #1745
*Jesse's Child #1776
*Chase's Promise #1791
*Trey's Secret #1823
***The Princess and the Cowboy* #1865

*The McClouds of Montana
†The Parks Empire
**The Hunt for Cinderella

LOIS FAYE DYER

lives in a small town on the shore of beautiful Puget Sound in the Pacific Northwest with her two eccentric and loveable cats, Chloe and Evie. She loves to hear from readers and you can write to her c/o Paperbacks Plus, 1618 Bay Street, Port Orchard, WA 98366. Visit her on the Web at www.LoisDyer.com and www.SpecialAuthors.com.

For Christine Flynn, Patricia Kay
and Allison Leigh—such good friends…

Prologue

Justin Hunt leaned against the library bookcase, one shoulder brushing a thick, leather-bound volume of Shakespeare. His fingers curled lightly around the narrow end of a pool cue, the heavier end of the cue resting on the floor. His Stetson lay on a nearby chair and his well-worn Levi's were faded above his dusty black cowboy boots. When he'd dressed at 4 a.m. to work cattle on his Idaho ranch, he hadn't expected he'd be summoned to Seattle for an emergency family meeting.

He tried to remember the last time he and his three brothers had gathered together here at their father's house. Had to be a month or more ago, he thought—probably on the night Harry had had his heart attack.

"Well, hell. Talk about out of practice," Gray said with disgust as he missed a shot, and the four ball rolled across the green felt instead of dropping into a pocket. "Looks like you're up, Justin."

Justin shoved away from the wall of glossy cherry-wood shelves and walked slowly around the antique pool table, gauging the position of the remaining balls. The entire room was brightly lit. A Tiffany lamp hung directly over the table's felt surface. A dozen or more sconces gleamed at regularly spaced intervals between the book-shelves lining the walls. Brass lamps glowed atop polished tables grouped with club chairs in comfortable, inviting seating areas on the oriental rugs. At the far end of the library was Harrison Hunt's mahogany desk. Cleverly recessed lighting in the boxed ceiling illuminated the glossy surface, the high-backed leather chair and the semicircle of straight-backed chairs before it. The desk faced the wall of windows and French doors that let out onto the patio overlooking the estate's private beach on Lake Washington. Across the lake, the Seattle skyline glowed against the night sky.

Justin leaned over the pool table. He'd long since grown accustomed to playing pool in the luxurious library because Harry had had the felt-covered table installed there when his sons were teenagers. His attempt to lure the boys into sharing the room with him while he worked from home had been successful but whether it resulted in a stronger parent-child relationship was up for debate.

In any event, Justin rarely noticed the opulent surroundings of his father's home. The high-tech mansion he and his brothers had dubbed "The Shack" as teenagers had been his home from the age of twelve until he'd left for college at eighteen. But tonight the familiar surroundings seemed to hold a sense of foreboding, as if the room held its breath, waiting.

"Does anybody know why the Old Man called

this meeting?" Justin asked as he tapped the six ball and watched it roll smoothly into the corner pocket.

Gray, the oldest of the brothers at forty-two, shrugged his shoulders. "My secretary said he wouldn't tell her the reason."

"Harry called you himself? Me, too." Sprawled in a deep leather armchair several feet from the pool table, the lanky six-foot-three Alex was Justin's closest brother in age. At thirty-six, he was only two years older than Justin. Alex waved his half-empty bottle of Black Sheep Ale at the fourth brother, seated in a matching armchair only a few feet away. "What about you, J.T.? Did you get the message from his secretary, or from Harry personally?"

Thirty-eight years old and as tall and lean as the rest of them, J.T. rubbed his eyes, yawned, and leaned forward. "From Harry." Elbows on his thighs, he held his tumbler of hundred-year-old Bourbon loosely in one hand. "I told him I'd have to cancel a week of meetings in New Delhi and spend half a day on the corporate jet to get home in time, but he insisted I be here." He ran his hand through his dark hair and looked at Justin. "What about you?"

"I was at the ranch when he called. He told me the same thing he told you—I had to be here. No excuses." Justin frowned, searching each of his brothers faces in turn. "He refused to tell me what the meeting was about. Did he tell any of you why he wanted to talk to us?"

"No." Gray shook his head, as did Alex and J.T.

Before Justin could respond, the hall door burst open and their father strode into the room. Harrison Hunt's six-foot-six frame was trim, his black hair barely showing any gray. Horn-rimmed bifocals framed his blue eyes but didn't conceal the intelligence of the man who'd invented the computer languages and software that had made HuntCom a household word. His energetic pace seemed miraculous after the heart attack that had felled him so recently.

"Ah, you're all here. Excellent." Harry waved his hand at his desk and moved briskly toward it. "Join me, boys."

Justin laid the pool cue on the table, settled his Stetson on his head, tugged the brim lower and followed Harry. Neither he nor his brothers took one of the chairs facing the big desk, choosing instead to remain standing. Justin hooked his thumbs in his front Levi pockets and leaned against the wall once more. He was almost, but not quite, out of Harrison's sight.

His father frowned at them all, swiveling his chair to stare at Justin. "Why don't you sit down?"

"Thanks, but I'll stand."

Harry swept the other three with the same frown.

Gray stood behind one of the chairs; Alex leaned against the wall by Gray while J.T. was separated from them all by the long credenza separating the seating areas.

Harry shrugged impatiently. "Very well. Stand or sit, it makes no difference to the outcome of this meeting." He cleared his throat. "Since my heart attack last month, I've been doing a lot of thinking about this family. I've never thought a lot about my legacy, nor to having grandchildren to carry on the Hunt name. However, the heart attack made me face some hard truths I'd ignored—I could have died. I could die tomorrow." He stood, rested his knuckles on the desktop and leaned forward, his face grimly intent. "I finally realized that, left to your own devices, you four never *will* get married, which means I'll never have grandchildren. I don't intend to leave the future of this family to chance any longer. You have a year. By the end of that year, each of you will not only be married, you will either already have a child or your wife will be expecting one."

The silence thickened, lengthened.

"Right," J.T. finally muttered, dryly.

Justin bit back a grin and looked past J.T. at Gray, noting the amusement flashing across his brother's face. To Gray's left, Alex merely lifted an eyebrow and sipped from his bottle of ale to drink.

"If any one of you refuses to do so," Harry continued, as if he hadn't noticed their lack of interest, "you'll all lose your positions in HuntCom and the perks you love so much."

Justin stiffened. *What the hell?*

Gray's face lost all amusement. "You can't be serious."

"I'm deadly serious."

"With all due respect, Harry," J.T. spoke, breaking the brief, stunned silence, "how will you run the company if we refuse to do this?" He gestured at his brothers. "I don't know what Gray, Alex or Justin have going on right now, but I'm in the middle of expansions here in Seattle, in Jansen and at our Delhi facility. If another architect has to take over my position, it'll be months before he's up to speed. Construction delays alone would cost HuntCom a fortune."

"It wouldn't matter, because if the four of you refuse to agree, I'll sell off HuntCom in pieces. The Delhi facility will be history, and I'll sell Hurricane Island." Harry's gaze left J.T. and met Justin's without flinching. "I'll sell HuntCom's interest in the Idaho ranch." He looked at Alex. "I'll shut down the foundation if you refuse to cooperate." Lastly, his hard stare met Gray's. "And HuntCom won't need a president because there will no longer be a company for you to run."

Gray's expression went stony.

"But that's insane," Alex said. "What do you hope to accomplish by doing this, Harry?"

"I mean to see you all settled with a family started before I die." Harry's eyes darkened. "With a decent woman who'll make a good wife and mother. The women you marry have to win Cornelia's approval."

"Does Aunt Cornelia know about this?" Justin found it hard to believe his honorary aunt, the widow of Harry's best friend, was a willing partner in his father's crazy scheme.

"Not yet."

Justin felt a surge of relief. When Cornelia learned what Harry was planning, she'd pitch a fit. She was the only one Harry was likely to listen to.

"So," Justin said slowly. "Let me see if I've got this straight. Each of us has to agree to marry and produce a kid within a year…"

"All of you have to agree," Harry interrupted. "All four of you. If one refuses, everyone loses, and life as you've known it—your jobs, the HuntCom holdings you each love—will be gone."

Justin ignored all three of his brothers' muttered curses and continued. "…and the brides have to each be approved by Aunt Cornelia."

Harry nodded. "She's a shrewd woman. She'll know if any of the women aren't good wife material. Which reminds me," he added abruptly. "You can't tell the women you're rich, or that you're my sons. I don't want any fortune hunters in the family. God knows, I married enough of those myself. I don't want any of my sons making the mistakes I made." He drew a deep breath. "I'll give you some time to think about this. You have until 8 p.m. Pacific time, three days from now. If I don't hear from you to the contrary before then, I'll tell my lawyer to start looking for a buyer for HuntCom."

He rounded the edge of the desk and left the room, the door closing quietly behind him.

The four watched him go with varying expressions of anger and disbelief.

"Son of a bitch," Justin said softly, his eyes narrowed in thought. "I think he means it."

Chapter One

Lily Spencer sipped her first cup of organic green tea while standing at the kitchen island of her town house, the pages of the *Seattle Times* spread out over the white marble counter in front of her. Early-morning sun spilled through the window behind her as she read, slowly turning the pages and enjoying the peaceful, quiet moments before her daughter awoke.

She skimmed the business articles and flipped the page to the Seattle Life section. A photo of a jogger at Green Lake was prominently featured at the top of the page.

Lily caught her breath, the gently steaming mug held motionless halfway to her lips. She narrowed her eyes and stared, trying to make out the man's features. But his face was partly turned away from the photographer.

Still, she knew with gut-deep conviction that the jogger was Justin Hunt. A gray tank top with a University of Washington logo left his broad shoulders and upper arms bare, the muscles of his thighs and long legs powerful beneath the hem of his black jogging shorts. Sunlight gleamed off sweat-dampened tanned skin.

She skimmed the brief caption beneath the photo, confirming her guess. The jogger was indeed Justin Hunt, in town for meetings the reporter speculated were important, since all four of the Hunt brothers had been seen in Seattle over the last twenty-four hours.

Lily leaned over the counter, her fingertips brushing the photo.

Then reality intruded and her lips firmed, compressing into a frown. She set her mug on the counter with a distinct clunk.

So he's back in town. So what?

She'd stopped jogging at Green Lake after Justin had dumped her. The wide asphalt track that circled the lake had been her favorite spot to run, but the possibility that she might see him, either alone or with another woman, wasn't one she cared to chance. Nowadays, she jogged along the waterfront, timing her visits to avoid the arrival of the cross-sound ferries and the wave of traffic from the passengers and vehicles they brought with them.

The baby monitor sitting on the counter next to the toaster crackled, followed by the subtler sound of rustling bedclothes.

Lily glanced at her wristwatch and smiled. Right on time, she thought.

"Ma-ma. Ma-ma." Ava's voice came clearly over the monitor.

Lily folded the newspaper and left the kitchen for her daughter's bedroom. Ava looked up the moment Lily opened the door. She grinned with obvious delight and held up her arms to her mother.

"Good morning, sweetie." Lily picked up the one-year-old toddler and cuddled her close. "Did you sleep well last night?"

Ava responded with a string of sounds interspersed with several "mamas," chortling when Lily nuzzled her downy cheek.

Lily carried Ava downstairs, tucked her into her highchair and shook a handful of Cheerios onto the tray. As Ava carefully picked them up, one by one, and tucked them into her mouth, Lily switched on the kettle for her daughter's morning oatmeal.

Justin is ancient history, she thought. *He's probably in town for a meeting at HuntCom, and will be gone soon.*

She picked up the newspaper and dropped it into the recycling bin, determined to forget the photo.

And Justin Hunt, as well.

Twenty-four hours after the meeting with Harry, Justin drove away from his aunt Cornelia's home in Queen Anne, dialed his cell phone and waited to be connected to his brothers. His conversation with Cornelia had convinced him there was a strong possibility Harry's threat to sell the company was real. Cornelia was growing increasingly worried by Harry's demeanor since the heart attack. Without prodding from Justin, she'd confided that Harry seemed uncharacteristically introspective. On several occasions, Harry had told her he wanted his sons to marry and have children. Cornelia was afraid Harry felt a need to right his wrongs, and that he was getting his fiscal and emotional affairs in order, preparing to die.

Privately, Justin thought the Old Man was too damned stubborn to die, but he didn't tell Cornelia that. She was one of the few women he actually respected, and she genuinely cared for Harry.

Of course, he thought, she'd known Harry since they were kids. They had years of history between them.

"Justin? What's up?" Gray spoke over a muted background of conversation and music.

"I've just left Cornelia's. I think we should take

the Old Man's deal," Justin said bluntly. "Here's why." With a few brief words, he told his brothers what Cornelia had told him. "I own sixty percent of the ranch and I want the rest of it. I'm not willing to chance Harry selling the other forty percent to anyone else."

"You're willing to let him choose your wife?" Alex's tone was pure disbelief.

"No. Cornelia convinced me the Old Man's heart attack might have scared him enough to believe he has to force us to marry and have kids for our own good," Justin said. "I'm willing to tell him that's what's happening until we've had time to figure a way around this, or he realizes how crazy his demand is. But in the meantime," Justin added, "I'll do what's necessary to keep him from selling the ranch. If that means looking for a wife, that's what I'll do."

"He's bluffing. He'd never sell the company," Gray said with conviction. "Even if he does hold the controlling interest."

Which is a damn shame, Justin thought. He and his brothers, together with Cornelia and her four daughters, all sat on the board, but even if they voted as a block, they couldn't override Harry.

"I don't see it happening," J.T. agreed. "He spent his life building HuntCom. We all know the company is more important to him than anything else, especially us. I don't believe he'd sacrifice it just to see us all married with babies." Derision laced his words.

"We're in the middle of a buyout," Gray said. "There's no way he'd consider selling the company until it's finished, and that might be months away. He's bluffing."

"How can you be sure?" Alex asked. "What if you're wrong? Do you want to chance losing everything you've worked for over the past eighteen years? I know I sure as hell don't want to see the foundation shut down...or run by someone else."

"The only baby Harry's every cared about is HuntCom. There's no way he won't do what's ultimately best for the company," Gray said. "He always does."

"I sure as hell hope you're right," Justin

muttered. "Where did he get the idea it was time we all went hunting for brides?"

"A Bride Hunt," J.T. grinned. "Sounds like one of those reality shows."

"Yeah," Alex put in dryly. "A really bad reality show."

"You know this won't work unless all of us are in," Gray said.

"And it won't work for any of us unless we come up with a contract that ties Harry's hands in the future," Justin added. "We have to make sure he can never blackmail us like this again."

"Absolutely," J.T. put in. "If he thinks he can manipulate us with threats, he'll do it again in a heartbeat."

"So we need an iron-clad contract that controls the situation." Justin could tell from J.T. and Alex's tones that they were considering whether to join him. He wasn't so sure about Gray. "If all Harry threatened us with was loss of income, I'd tell him to go to hell, and walk. But I'm not willing to lose the ranch. Nor do I want to be the cause of another heart attack that might kill him. What about the rest of you?"

The brief silence that followed his question was finally broken by Alex. "If it was just money, I'd tell him to go to hell, too. But it's not, is it?"

"It's about the things and places he knows matter most to us." J.T. sounded grim.

"Part of Harry's demand was that the brides not know our identity until after we're married. How are you going to find an eligible woman in Seattle who doesn't know you're rich, Justin?" Gray asked.

"I've been out of state for most of the last two years, plus I've never been as high profile as the rest of you."

"Yeah, right," J.T. scoffed. "There isn't a single one of us who hasn't had our picture in the paper or in a magazine."

"But not as often as Harry," Gray said thoughtfully. "He's the public face of HuntCom. I've got to give the Old Man credit, he's deflected as much publicity from us as he could."

"True," Justin agreed. "So, how about it, Gray? Are you in?"

"Face it, Gray," Alex said. "Harry holds all the cards."

"He always has." J.T. sighed audibly.

"Okay, fine," Gray finally said. "But the only way to tie the Old Man's hands is by outvoting him in the boardroom. I'm not agreeing to *anything* without an iron-clad agreement, *in writing,* that he'll transfer enough voting shares to each of us so that he can't pull this again the next time he gets some wild hair. If we can't back out, neither can he. Nor can he start adding on more conditions just because he feels like it. The only thing he's ever understood is HuntCom. Once he's no longer squarely in the driver's seat, *then* I'll start believing he's really concerned about us passing on the family name—no matter how concerned Cornelia seemed."

Justin rang off, dropping the cell phone onto the seat next to him. He'd never wanted to get married, let alone have a kid.

If Harry expected hearts and flowers with some sappy version of true love along with Justin's cooperation, the Old Man was in for a rude awakening. Hell, Harry's threats and demands were downright bizarre.

The morning after the conference call with his brothers, Justin woke early. Just before 6 a.m., he carried a mug of coffee, a writing pad and a pen out to the deck. Several streets below, sunlight sparkled on the waters of Puget Sound. An ocean freighter lumbered slowly through the deep water toward the Port of Tacoma to the south. Its ponderous size and speed made the boxy white-and-green Washington State ferry appear sprightly and swift as it neared Colman Dock on the Seattle waterfront.

Much as he loved his Idaho ranch, Justin couldn't deny the Pacific Northwest was stunningly beautiful on this sunny July morning. He tipped his chair back, propped his bare feet on the seat of a neighboring chair, ankles crossed, and wrote a name in capital letters at the top of his potential-bride list.

Lily Spencer.

She probably never wants to see me again, he thought, remembering the Tiffany bracelet she'd returned the morning after he'd broken off their affair. The box was unopened, his note still sealed in its envelope. The messenger who brought back the items had told his secretary Lily herself had written Return To Sender in black script across the front of the envelope.

Justin had left Seattle the next day and had rarely returned over the following two years. Long days spent in punishing physical labor had exhausted his body but hadn't stopped his mind from thinking about her. Finally, after months of pain, the ache in his chest where his heart was went numb. He figured that meant he was finally over her.

But you haven't stopped thinking about her. You haven't forgotten her.

He tuned out the small voice in his head and went back to his list-making, forcing himself to write despite the distaste he felt for the task.

He jotted down the names of three unmarried women before he stopped abruptly, frowning at the list. Every one of them was a business connection he'd met through HuntCom. They all knew he was billionaire Harry Hunt's son.

How the hell am I going to find a bride if they can't know who I am?

Despite equating the Bride Hunt with any other project he'd done for HuntCom, Justin felt a distinct reluctance to make the very personal details of Harry's demand known outside the family.

I suppose I could use a pseudonym and join an online dating service. Almost immediately, he dismissed the thought. *Too time-consuming.*

He stared at the rooftops—marching in neat blocks down the hill between him and the waterfront—while he considered the problem.

He drank his coffee and watched the marine traffic on the waterfront, his thoughts drifting back to Lily Spencer. He ended his relationship with Lily when he'd realized she was a woman who wanted marriage and a family. Neither of those two commitments were in his future. He'd walked away from her so she could find what she needed.

He punched in the phone number for her shop, frowning as he realized he still remembered it, even though he hadn't dialed it in years.

"Good morning, Princess Lily Boutique. How may I help you?"

"Is Lily in?"

"May I ask who's calling?"

"Justin Hunt."

"One moment, please."

Justin paced impatiently, listening to the murmur of female voices and occasional laughter in the background.

"I'm sorry, Mr. Hunt." When she finally came back on the line, the feminine voice was distinctly cooler than before. "Ms. Spencer isn't available."

"When do you expect her?"

"I'm afraid I don't know," she said politely. "May I take a message?"

"No message." Justin hung up, convinced the woman was lying.

He suspected Lily was somewhere in the shop or in her workroom one floor above, but had refused to take his call.

When he'd abruptly ended their three-month affair, Lily hadn't cried or called him names. Unlike other women he'd dated and broken things off with, Lily hadn't made a scene at the restaurant. Instead, she'd carefully folded her napkin, stood and walked out without a word.

Maybe that was another reason he needed to see her—maybe he wanted her to yell at him and tell him what a rat he was for dumping her. Then he could apologize, and if he was lucky, she'd forgive him. At least then she wouldn't hate him for the rest of her life.

With sudden decisiveness, he grabbed his keys from the counter and left the apartment. Ten minutes later, he parked the Escalade on Ballard Avenue and jogged across the brick street, dodging traffic.

The mannequins in the bowfront display windows of Lily's shop wore white lace bustiers and garter belts, and were posed against draped black satin. Justin stepped inside, the shop's interior an Aladdin's cave of jewel-tone colors and sexy silk and lace women's underwear. The air had a subtle floral scent, and the designs and textures of the lingerie were extravagantly feminine.

The door eased shut behind him and he paused,

searching the room. Everywhere he looked, he was reminded of Lily.

Several women browsed the racks and shelves. All of them gave him curious glances. He ignored them, scanning the shop, hoping to find Lily. She wasn't there.

"May I help you, sir?" The willowy redhead behind the counter left a customer sifting through a basket of lacy thongs and approached him.

Justin recognized her voice; she was the woman he'd talked to on the phone earlier.

"I'm looking for Lily."

The redhead's eyes widened, her smile disappearing. "I'm sorry, sir. She isn't in."

"When do you expect her?"

"I'm not sure. Would you care to leave a message?"

"Yeah, sure." He took a card from his pocket and jotted his cell-phone number on the back, followed by the words *call me.*

The salesclerk took the card and glanced at it. "No other message?" Her expression was sharply curious.

"No."

"I'll make sure she gets the card."

"Thanks," Justin drawled, suspecting his card would hit the trash can as soon as he left the shop. He wondered if Lily was upstairs in her workroom, avoiding him.

Short of forcing his way through the Employees Only door behind the counter and climbing the stairs, he couldn't be sure. And he didn't want to go there—there were other ways to reach her.

Tonight he'd drive to Lily's town house and knock on her door unannounced. He'd apologize for ending their affair, make sure she was having a happy life, ask her to forgive him and leave.

He left the shop and waited for a break in traffic before crossing the street to his SUV.

Not being able to contact Lily easily had made him even more determined to see her.

Justin drove back to his apartment and forced himself to wait until evening, giving Lily plenty of time to go home before he sought her out.

Lily lived in Ballard, an older but upwardly mobile community edging the waters of Puget

Sound just north of downtown Seattle. The newer brick-and-wood building was split into six town houses, each with a small square of grass out front.

Rush hour and dinnertime were past and the neighborhood was quiet, with only an occasional jogger accompanied by their dog, or a young couple pushing a stroller along the sidewalk passing by.

The walkway to Lily's home was swept clean and edged with flower beds filled with red Martha Washington geraniums and green ferns. Justin rang the doorbell, idly noting the small, tidy porch with its wicker bench and the dried herb wreath that hung on the wall above it.

The minutes dragged by. Impatient, he pushed the button again, the ring of the chimes muted through the thick door.

Maybe she's not home. Disappointed and frustrated, Justin half turned to search the quiet street, but saw no one. In a last attempt before leaving, he turned back and pushed the bell one more time.

The door opened abruptly.

"What?" The single word was filled with annoyance. A frown veed sable brows above green eyes that widened, flaring with shocked surprise as Lily stared at him.

Deep inside Justin, something that had been unsettled calmed, the emptiness that had been his constant companion for months eased and filled. His memory hadn't betrayed him. The green eyes, high cheekbones and lush mouth, with its full lower lip, were exactly as he'd remembered. Lily's shoulder-length hair was tousled, the sunlight glinting off streaks of blond in the dark brown mane. His gaze moved lower and, belatedly, he realized she wasn't alone.

A little girl perched on Lily's hip. Her tiny shoulders and arms were bare above the blue towel wrapped around her torso and her chubby little legs and feet left damp spots on Lily's shorts. The toddler's coal-black hair clung to her cheeks and nape in damp curls. Her green eyes were framed with thick black lashes, and when she smiled at him, a dimple flashed in her cheek next to a rosebud mouth.

The toddler had Lily's eyes. And his hair and dimple.

He dragged his gaze from the little girl and met Lily's. Emotions chased across her expressive features—surprise replaced by a swift look of guilt that was quickly banished by the defiant lift of her chin.

Then she slammed the door shut.

Chapter Two

Shock held Justin paralyzed for one stunned moment before he pounded on the door panels. "Lily!"

"Go away!"

"Open the door or I'll keep this up until your neighbors call the cops."

The door flew open. "What do you want?" she demanded.

"Let me in."

"No."

"Do you really want to have this conversation on your doorstep?" he asked grimly.

Her gaze flickered over his shoulder and a small, forced smile lifted the corners of her mouth. She waved. "Hi, Mrs. Baker. Nice evening, isn't it?" She stepped back and held the door. wide. "Come in," she hissed at Justin.

The moment he stepped over the threshold, she closed the door and quickly moved farther into the room to put space between them.

"What are you doing here?" she demanded.

"I'm in town. I wanted to say hello," Justin said almost absently, shock still gripping him. He couldn't take his eyes off the little girl. "What's her name?"

"Ava." Lily gathered the toddler closer, her stance protective. "You've said hello, now I want you to leave."

"Oh, no." He shook his head. He wasn't sure of much, since his brain felt as if it had been scrambled by a bolt of lightning, but he did know he wasn't leaving. Not yet. "Not until you tell me about Ava. She's mine, isn't she." It wasn't a question. He was convinced he knew what Lily's answer would be, but he wanted, needed, to hear her say the words.

"No, she's not yours. She's mine."

"Mama." Ava patted Lily's cheek, demanding her attention. "Mine Mama."

"Yes, sweetie, I'm your mama. And you're my very best girl, aren't you."

Ava threw her arms around Lily's neck and hugged her enthusiastically. Then she laid her head on her mother's shoulder and smiled beatifically at Justin.

His heart stuttered and he couldn't help smiling helplessly back at her.

"She's mine," he said softly, but with rock-solid conviction.

"You contributed DNA, but that doesn't make her yours."

Lily's vehement words were more denial than confirmation, but Justin's heart leapt just the same. He'd felt numb for the last two years, and the pound of his heart in his chest after so long was startling.

"I want you to leave," Lily said quietly.

"We need to talk."

"No, we don't. There's nothing to discuss. Ava and I have a life. You're not part of it. Go away." Her voice was a shade less quiet, and a faint tremor shook her.

Ava's smile disappeared. She looked from Justin to her mother, then back again, her little face concerned. "Mama?"

"Please go. This is upsetting Ava."

"All right, I'll leave." Justin kept his voice even, his tone mild. "But we have to talk. I'll call you at the shop in the morning."

She didn't answer. Instead, she merely nodded, then walked to the door and held it open, closing it silently behind him.

Lily stared at the door. She was shaking, tremors of shock and anger rippling in waves from her midsection through to her arms and into her fingertips. She'd never expected Justin to show up on her doorstep. He must have known Meggie was lying to him when he'd telephoned and then dropped by the shop.

There had to be dozens of women listed in his little black book who would be delighted to take his calls. Why did he have to come looking for her? If she'd thought there was any possibility he wouldn't move on to greener pastures after he was unable to reach her earlier, she would have been more careful. She certainly wouldn't have opened her front door with Ava in her arms.

Lily squeezed her eyes shut, trying to erase the image of him standing on her doorstep. He wore polished black cowboy boots, and worn Levi's covered his long legs and powerful thighs. His pale blue cotton shirt screamed designer-label and she was sure the gold watch on his wrist was a Rolex. When he'd smiled at Ava, dimples dented the tanned skin of his cheeks. With his coal-black hair, piercing blue eyes and muscled body, honed by jogging and long hours working on the Idaho ranch he loved, Justin Hunt was every woman's dream.

Except mine, she thought fiercely. *Justin Hunt is my own personal nightmare.* And contrary to her assumptions, he seemed entranced by Ava.

The possibility that he might have wanted to know she'd become pregnant with his baby was unacceptable. And frankly terrifying. She shuddered, unwilling to consider that she might have misjudged him.

Ava wiggled, babbling a protest, and Lily realized she was clutching her too tightly.

"I'm sorry, honey," she crooned, brushing a kiss against the toddler's quickly drying curls. "Mama didn't mean to scrunch you." She shifted Ava higher, the little body a warm, reassuring weight against her chest. "Let's go put your jammies on and find a book to read before your bedtime, okay?"

Ava responded with her own babbled version of English, her unintelligible sentences liberally sprinkled with "Mama."

Lily distracted herself with Ava's nighttime rituals of donning pajamas and reading two Sandra Boynton books with Lily, then she dimmed the lights for fifteen minutes of cuddling in the rocking chair before tucking the sleepy little girl into her crib.

But when she went back downstairs, the house

quiet about her, there was no escaping the flood of memories Justin's visit had caused.

One rainy evening a little over two years ago, Justin had walked into a florist's shop in downtown Seattle. She'd been there, ordering flowers to cheer a hospitalized friend. While he'd waited to give the clerk his order, they'd chatted. The attraction between them was instant and mutual. They'd flirted, then went next door to share dinner, after which she'd refused his offer of a ride and driven herself home. It wasn't until the next day that she'd made the connection between his name and the huge HuntCom corporation that was a Seattle household word.

When he'd called and asked her out that afternoon, she'd told him she wasn't sure she should date one of the playboy Hunt brothers, but he'd laughed and charmed her into agreeing to meet him.

With Justin, she'd broken every rule she'd ever had about caution with men in relationships. She'd let her heart overrule her head and had swiftly fallen head over heels in love with him. He was handsome, sexy, charming and very, very rich. But she'd never indulged in casual sex. Nevertheless, he'd quickly overwhelmed her reservations and within a week, they were sleeping together. Once in his bed, she was committed. When he'd abruptly broken off their relationship, she'd been devastated.

The night he told her goodbye over dinner, she'd been so stunned by his words she hadn't responded, had been incapable of speech. She'd managed to stand, leave the restaurant and catch a cab for home.

She didn't leave her house for a week, grappling with heartbreak. Then she'd gone back to work, determined to put her life back together.

And I did. Lily pulled herself out of memories, shaking off the sadness that always accompanied remembering those dark days after Justin left. *He broke my heart once. I don't want him in my life again. I don't need Justin Hunt.*

She walked into the living room, bending to pick up several of Ava's toys scattered across the rug and tossing them into the wicker toy basket beneath the window.

Her life was organized and on track, she reminded herself firmly. Because she had her own shop, she could take Ava to work with her, and she'd turned an empty office space into a nursery. She spent most of her time in the second-floor workroom with Ava nearby, working on the design and production phases of her business, while trusted staff ran her boutique below. Business was booming, and only last month, an article in the *Seattle Times* about the local fashion industry had called her a rising star, and dubbed her a true "Princess" Lily.

It's taken a long time to get my life back on track. The last thing I want is to let Justin disrupt it again.

Except—he's Ava's father.

The thought brought her to a standstill, motionless in the center of the cozy living room, with a stuffed teddy bear in one hand and a doggie pull-toy in the other.

What if he wants to take Ava? She'd never considered the possibility that Justin might want custody. But she'd recognized the smile he'd given

Ava. She suspected she had that same love-struck expression when she looked at her daughter. Smitten, she thought. He'd looked hopelessly smitten.

While she could understand why anyone would fall in love with her precious daughter, the possibility Justin had done so was not to be contemplated. His obvious interest in her little girl opened whole new vistas of worry.

Not only was Justin wealthy in his own right, he also had access to power through his billionaire father.

She dropped onto the sofa cushion, frowning unseeingly at the forgotten toys in her hand. She needed a professional opinion, she decided. She'd call her attorney first thing in the morning.

Fighting the urge to pack her bags, bundle Ava into her car and flee Seattle, she rose and finished picking up the scattered toys before retreating to her workroom just off the kitchen. She spent the next few hours trying to focus on an exclusive design for a client in Hollywood.

She thought she'd dealt successfully with Justin's sudden reappearance in her life. But when she went to bed just after ten-thirty, she couldn't fall asleep. She spent the next eight hours alternately turning, tossing and infrequently dozing.

He was haunting her dreams once again.

Justin drove home in a daze.

He'd had to force himself to walk down the sidewalk and get in the SUV. Every instinct in him demanded he stay with Lily and the little girl she held in her arms.

He had a daughter. The concept shook him to the core.

He never would have guessed that one look at a dainty little female with her mama's eyes and his own black hair would have knocked him off balance.

"I'm a father." Even spoken aloud, the words seemed surreal. He'd walked away from a relationship with Lily to keep from harming her, but he'd left her to have his baby alone. *Bad move. Really bad move. I should have made sure she was okay,* he thought, filled with self-anger and disgust. *I should have protected her.*

He didn't know a damn thing about kids, let alone babies. And he knew even less about being a father. His mother had hooked up with several men during the twelve years he'd lived with her. None of them had been interested in being a father-figure. At best, they'd ignored him. At worst, he'd earned curses and slaps. He'd learned early to avoid the ones who used their fists. They'd taught him plenty about survival but nothing about being a good parent.

At least Harry had never hit him or his brothers, he thought. The Old Man had been absorbed with HuntCom, sometimes to the extent that Justin wondered if he remembered he had sons in the house. But he never purposely abused or neglected them. There was always food on the table, adults hired to keep track of them and clean clothing without holes.

All in all, Harry hadn't been such a bad father. Just…not really *there*.

Harry. What the hell am I going to do about Harry and his rules for the Bride Hunt? The thought shocked him out of his musings, and he realized he'd driven from Ballard to downtown Seattle on autopilot. Seeing Lily with Ava had changed everything, he realized.

Beyond talking to Lily in the morning, he wasn't sure what his next step would be. One thing he did know—he had to put his part in the Bride Hunt on hold.

The sun had set and streetlights winked on as he reached Second Avenue and turned south toward his penthouse apartment above a HuntCom building in Pioneer Square. The roar of a capacity crowd watching the Mariners play baseball in Safeco Field reminded him he'd left the quiet of his Idaho ranch behind.

A half block from his building, he hit a button on the dash, and by the time he'd turned into the underground parking lot, the gates were open. They eased silently shut behind him. Moments later, he stepped off the elevator and into the company apartment he called home whenever he was in Seattle.

He flicked on the television, removed his boots and dropped onto the sofa, propping his feet on the coffee table.

The Seattle newscaster warned motorists about the usual traffic backup on Interstate 5. Justin switched channels, clicking absentmindedly through the cable offerings, barely registering them.

He was unable to concentrate on anything beyond the mind-numbing news that he and Lily had a daughter. He turned off the TV and paced the high-ceilinged area of the big loft, but his mind continued to spin.

He'd never planned to marry or have children for very good reasons. There was no way a man with his background would make a competent, solid husband or father. He'd never been exposed to normal family dynamics, and had no clue what to do to create them.

That's why he'd broken off his relationship with Lily in the first place. Justin slid open the glass doors and stepped out onto the wide deck that ran the length of the apartment. He walked past the hot tub and the teak patio table and chairs, all covered with white canvas. The summer night was balmy, and he sat on the wide brick balustrade.

He couldn't stop thinking about Lily and Ava.

And about the unlikely odds that a man with his past wouldn't end up harming them both.

He'd come to live with Harry in Seattle when he was twelve, but Justin had always preferred the far-flung acres of the ranch in Idaho. He'd lived all over the world with his mother and an ever-changing series of her men friends until he was eight. Then she'd dumped him at the ranch with his grandfather, who was the foreman of the sprawling property. When the elderly man died four years later, his wife contacted Harry, and within twenty-four hours, the billionaire had arrived with his eldest son, Gray. Justin didn't want to leave the only stable home he'd ever know, and when Harry told him to pack his belongings to return to Seattle, he'd disappeared into the mountains on horseback. He'd planned to outwait the businessman, but Harry sent Gray with a ranchhand to find him, making an offer he couldn't refuse. He'd left Idaho for the Hunt family compound in the exclusive Seattle suburb of Medina with the guarantee that someday he'd own the ranch, free and clear.

It was a promise Harry had kept—at least partially. Justin now owned sixty percent of the land he loved, having worked, invested and bought the acres from Harry.

Harry's sudden interest in marriage and grandkids didn't make sense, especially since his own marriages had been disasters of near Biblical proportions. He'd married four beautiful women, and every one of them had turned out to be interested only in his money. Justin's own mother had told him she'd married Harry because of his billions, and then purposely gotten pregnant. She'd planned to collect millions in return for granting Harry full custody, as his earlier wives had done. Unfortunately, Harry hadn't believed she was pregnant, and after a furious argument, she'd walked out. She was so vengeful that she'd kept Justin's existence a secret from Harry for twelve years. Long enough for his mother's lifestyle of rich men and wild parties to leave an indelible mark on Justin's life.

None of which makes any difference now, Justin thought. Except, given Harry's history with women who'd turned out to be disasters as wives and mothers, Justin couldn't help wondering why his father would want any of his sons to marry.

Not to mention the fact that Harry himself hadn't been anyone's candidate for father of the year, Justin thought. Running a software company that grew at the speed of light, coupled with the hours Harry spent developing software innovations, pretty much ate up the waking hours of each day. There had been no Beaver Cleaver family moments in the Hunt household, no father and son bonding while tossing a football or baseball in the backyard. Harry rarely made it to school conferences or sporting events. Fortunately, when her girls were little and the Fairchilds were in town, Cornelia and her four daughters were faithful attendees at every public event.

There's no getting around it, Justin thought grimly. *I haven't got a clue how to be a husband or father. The learning curve to become barely competent has to be ninety degrees straight up from where I am.*

The wail of a sax drifted up from the jazz club a block away. The song was one of Lily's favorites. They'd danced to its slow, seductive rhythm at the same club a dozen or more times during the three months they'd spent together.

The sultry music stirred memories of those unforgettable nights. Justin felt as if Lily's soft, seductive hands were stroking his bare skin with every pulse of the music.

Abruptly, he left the deck to head inside for bed.

Lily dressed with extra care the next morning, changing her mind a dozen times before she settled on a cream linen business suit with a silk green tank top, three-inch sling-back pumps and a chunky gold watch and earrings.

She'd reached her attorney at 8:30 a.m., and their phone conversation had confirmed her worst fears. Justin had a legal right to be involved in Ava's life, should he wish to do so. She could choose whether she wanted to fight him in court or voluntarily attempt to work out a reasonable solution. The attorney had strongly advised her to seek an amicable agreement, especially given that the man involved was Justin Hunt.

Despite her resolve to never let Justin into her life again, it seemed she had no choice. But no matter what, she had to protect her little girl.

A little before ten, she left Ava in her nursery just off the workroom, playing happily with one of the seamstresses. Lily opened her umbrella and quickly walked down Ballard Avenue and crossed the wet brick pavement to the restaurant where she'd agreed to meet Justin for coffee. She was determined to remain calm, businesslike and focused on Ava.

She'd purposely chosen to meet him midmorning in hopes the breakfast trade would have left and the lunch crowd wouldn't start arriving for another hour or more. The restaurant was one where she often met clients for lunch meetings, and she was familiar with its semiprivate seating. While she certainly wanted a measure of privacy, she didn't want the intimacy of seeing Justin at either of their homes. The restaurant seemed a good compromise.

Justin had arrived before her and he stood as she neared the table.

"Hello, Lily."

"Good morning." Unfortunately, her determination to remain distant and unaffected disappeared the moment she saw him. He wore a long-sleeved shirt, the perfect fit obviously custom-tailored. The cuffs were turned back, the white cotton a stark contrast to his tanned skin at his forearms and collar. A silver-buckled black belt was threaded through the loops of his jeans, and polished black cowboy boots covered his feet. Raindrops dampened the shoulders of his shirt and gleamed in his dark hair. Unlike her, he apparently hadn't bothered with an umbrella.

He held her chair and she caught the subtle hint of his cologne as she took a seat. The familiar male scent brought with it a wash of unwanted memories. Her heart stuttered and she drew in a silent deep breath.

"I spoke with my attorney this morning," she said, determined to set a brisk tone to the meeting, as he took his own seat across from her.

"Did you?" he said, his face inscrutable as he surveyed her.

"Yes." She waited until the waiter had filled their cups and left a carafe of coffee before she continued. "Evidently, ours is not an unusual situation."

"It is to me," he replied. "I've never had a child before Ava."

"I meant the circumstance of having a child together without being married," Lily said evenly. "He's handled a lot of cases for couples with this issue."

"I see." Justin sat easily in his chair, his noncommital expression giving no indication as to what he was thinking. "And what advice did your attorney give you?"

"He recommended we focus on Ava and what's best for her."

"And you agree with that?"

"Yes, of course." Lily wished she knew what he was thinking. She lifted her cup and eyed him over the rim. "Do you agree?"

"Absolutely." His reply was prompt, with no hesitation.

"Good." She smiled with relief. "I'm delighted to hear that."

She hesitated, gathered her courage, and cut to the heart of the matter. "Now that you know you have a daughter, Justin, what do you plan to do about it, if anything?"

"I'm not sure, exactly. I think we should start with my getting to know her."

"You mean, you want to visit?"

"I suppose 'visit' is as good a term as any." He leaned forward. "I want to spend time with her. I've missed the first year of her life, Lily. Don't you think getting acquainted is long overdue?" A faint hint of anger surfaced.

"The night you ended our…affair, you made it very clear you weren't interested in marriage or children." She met his gaze without flinching. "Don't try to make me the bad guy here, Justin. It never occurred to me you'd want to know I was pregnant or that we had a daughter. In fact, just the opposite. Your words were very convincing—I believed you. If you didn't mean them, you shouldn't have said them."

He stared at her for a long moment before he shrugged. "You're right. I should have made it clear that if you learned you were pregnant, I wanted to know. When did you find out?"

"A few weeks after we broke up. I thought about telling you, but then I remembered your breakup speech. It seemed very clear to me that you had no interest in any commitment, including having a child."

"I didn't, then."

Lily searched his face. "And now?"

His eyes darkened. "Kids were never in my plan, Lily. But seeing Ava with you last night…" He paused, as if searching for words. "Let's just say she's changed all the rules. I'm her father. That means something to me, something important. I want to be a part of her life."

"Just how involved do you want to be?"

"Can't we start out slow? I'd like to spend time with her. Do you have any objections?"

A million, she thought. Remember what the attorney said, Lily told herself. If you refuse to let him visit Ava, he can sue you for visitation, or custody. "I can live with you getting to know her," she said, carefully evasive.

"Good." Justin appeared relieved. "When can we start?"

Lily wanted to name a date weeks away but knew she shouldn't delay the inevitable. *The sooner he's exposed to toddler-world reality, the faster he's likely to get bored and bow out of our lives.* "How about tomorrow? We're usually home by four o'clock and Ava goes to bed between seven and seven-thirty. If you'd like to come by around four-thirty, you can read to her while I make dinner."

"I'll be there. Can I bring anything?"

"Just your patience," she said dryly.

Chapter Three

"I thought you were only bringing your 'patience' tonight," Lily commented when she greeted Justin promptly at four-thirty that afternoon.

"I was downtown earlier and walked by a toy store. I couldn't resist going in," he explained. He carried a huge stuffed teddy bear under one arm; its soft plush brushed her arm as he stepped past her and into the small foyer. He handed her a bouquet of summer blooms, wrapped in green florist paper.

"Were these in the toy store, too?" She lowered her face to the flowers, closing her eyes as she inhaled.

"No, I got them at the Gazebo. That's why I went downtown." The bouquet was a mixture of lilies, soft pink roses, white baby's breath and lavender, with feathery green ferns. He'd asked the florist to put together the flowers he remembered she especially liked. And without consciously planning to, he'd gone to the Gazebo because that was where they'd first met.

"Oh. That was, um…" She faltered before visibly gathering herself. "They're lovely, thank you," she murmured, her green eyes darkened to jade when she looked up at him.

"You're welcome," Justin replied, distracted by the sight of her soft lips and skin next to the lush rose petals. He'd brushed his thumb over one of the pink blooms earlier; he knew her lips and skin were just as velvety soft, just as fragrant.

"Mama!" Ava's clear voice lifted in demand, ending the brief moment.

"Come in," Lily said over her shoulder as she

moved quickly away. "I can't leave Ava alone for more than a couple of seconds," she explained as he followed her. They crossed the living room and entered a family room/dining room/kitchen-combo space. Light and airy, the far end of the open room held counters, sink, stove and fridge arranged in a U-shape around a tiled island. Directly in front of them was the living space with a comfortable sofa, matching club chair with ottoman, and cherry-wood armoire that held a media center.

The furniture was arranged around an Oriental area rug centered on the polished hardwood floor. In the middle of the cream, red and brown wool rug was Ava.

The little girl sat in some sort of kiddie seat that looked like a round play table fastened to a plastic saucer base. She held a rattle in one hand and was busily pounding it on the hard plastic tabletop.

"Mama, Mama!" she chanted, smiling with toothless delight when she caught sight of Lily.

"Hi, sweetie." Lily laid the bouquet on the white marble tile of the island counter and returned to lift Ava. Her chubby little feet, bare beneath a pink cotton romper, tangled in the cotton seat and she kicked herself free.

Justin watched, fascinated, as Lily kissed the little girl, gave her a hug and settled the toddler on her hip before walking toward him.

"Look, Ava," she pointed at him. "Mommy's… friend, Justin is here to play with you. Isn't that nice?"

Ava ducked her head, suddenly shy, and clung to her mother while eyeing him from behind the shield of her amazingly long eyelashes.

Her fingers closed in a tiny fist, clutching a handful of Lily's white tank top. Her grip tugged the cotton neckline lower, exposing a strip of white lace covering the upper swell of Lily's breasts, and the shadow of the valley between. With an effort Justin dragged his gaze away from that tantalizing glimpse of bra and soft skin, and focused on the little girl.

"Hello, Ava," he said gravely, unsure as to what he was supposed to do. It seemed a little odd to be talking to a baby when he had no idea if she understood what he was saying.

"Look, Justin brought you a teddy bear." Lily touched the soft fur of the stuffed bear. "Ooh, he's so soft. Would you like to touch, Ava?"

She nodded and Lily stepped nearer, easing Ava close enough to smooth one small, dimpled hand over the thick brown pile.

He breathed in Lily's perfume as she stood in front of him, all her attention on Ava and the stuffed bear. The subtle fragrance she wore raised an instant mental image of kissing her bare skin while whey made love, the spicy feminine scent flooding his senses. A swift surge of arousal caught him off guard. Ruthlessly, he slammed the door on memories and thanked God Lily seemed unaware of his reaction.

"Isn't that nice?" Lily asked.

Ava nodded her head and petted the bear's arm once again, a small, pleased smile curving her mouth.

"Would you like to play with him?" Lily asked.

Ava nodded once more.

"Okay, Justin and the bear can sit with us." Lily lowered herself to the floor, Ava in her arms, and cradled the toddler on her lap. "Justin, why don't you join us."

"Right." Feeling as awkward as a whale out of water, Justin sat cross-legged on the carpet, facing the little girl who was holding out her arms expectantly.

He handed over the bear, grinning as she clutched it. The stuffed animal was taller than her, wider, and much too big for her arms to reach around its body. Nevertheless, she managed to hold on and rock side to side, crowing in approval.

"I think she likes it," he said.

Lily smiled. "I think it's safe to say she loves it. Oops." She leaned sideways to avoid getting smacked with one of the plush arms. "Would you like to sit over here with your bear?"

She lifted Ava and the bear off her lap, sitting the little girl down on her diaper-padded bottom. Ava immediately lost her balance and rolled sideways, taking the bear with her and chortling with delight.

"Is she always this happy?" Justin asked, glancing at Lily. Her face was soft, a half smile curving her mouth as she watched Ava with the stuffed toy.

"No, she had a late nap so she's rested at the moment. If she's tired or hungry or has a wet diaper or…any number of things, she can get very cranky, very fast. Generally speaking, though, she has a fairly even temperament."

"She must get that from you," Justin said wryly.

"Were you a difficult baby?" Lily asked.

"I have no idea." Justin shrugged. His mother hadn't said what he'd been like as a baby, but since he was old enough to remember, she'd told him he was in the way. He assumed the two went hand in hand.

Ava pushed away from the bear and began to crawl across the rug, her attention focused intently on a TV remote control lying on the sofa table.

"No, Ava." Lily stood and swept Ava up in her arms. "Would you read to Ava while I get her dinner ready? The books are over there." She pointed to a basket in the corner near the sofa.

"Sure." He rolled to his feet, selected several

small, hard-paged books with brightly colored covers, and walked back to Lily.

"Have a seat." Lily pointed at the club chair. "I'm not sure she'll sit with you, she's often shy with strangers, but we can try."

He put the books on the lamp table by the chair and held out his arms to take Ava. She eyed him for a moment before she launched herself at him, surprising both Justin and Lily.

"Well," Lily said. "I guess she's agreeable."

Justin gingerly balanced Ava on his lap and opened the book. The story was about birthday monsters, both clever and surprisingly funny. Each time he turned a page, Ava chattered with excitement and smacked her little hand on the colorful illustrations.

Ava's small body was a warm, solid weight in his arms.

She smelled like soap, baby power and some scent he couldn't identify. He wondered if all babies smelled this good or if it was unique to his daughter.

His experience with babies was zero, and the

amount of information he didn't know suddenly seemed gigantic.

She twisted to look up at him, chattering emphatically before pausing to eye him expectantly.

"Uh, yeah, sure." He had no idea what she'd just said, but his response seemed to satisfy her since she turned back to the book and pointed at the drawing of a grinning monster that bore a striking resemblance to a purple hippopotamus in a green fedora. "You like that one?"

Ava nodded vigorously and gave him an approving smile.

He grinned back at her, ridiculously pleased that he must have done something right. She chose that moment to lean back against his chest, going boneless in a display of trust that literally stole his breath. He was blindsided by a flood of emotions.

He glanced up, sure that Lily must have felt the floor shift beneath their feet, too, but she was at the kitchen counter and had her back to them while she stirred something in a small bowl.

It's just me, he thought. Maybe this happens with Lily everyday and she's grown used to it. *So this is what it's like to be a father,* he thought. Scared to death at how tiny and vulnerable your daughter is, wanting to protect her from the world, and so damned amazed at what a miracle she is.

Ava squirmed and sat up, patting the open book and chattering.

"Oops, sorry, Ava." Justin started reading again and Ava settled back, content to listen. They read four books and were starting a fifth before Lily interrupted them.

"Time for Ava's dinner."

Two hours later, Justin drove home after Lily reluctantly agreed he could return the following evening. He had a whole new perspective on parenthood. *How did Lily do that every night by herself?*

No wonder she's in great shape, he thought. Ava's nonstop whirlwind of activity required constant supervision and he'd watched Lily lift the solid little body dozens of times. *I bet she never has to hit the gym. She's got her own personal weightlifting program with Ava.*

The toddler was amazing—and so was Lily. He'd planned to remain a lifelong bachelor until

Harry's ultimatum. Even when he'd agreed to marry, he'd meant to offer a wife a business arrangement only. All that had changed, he realized, because now that he knew about Ava and had seen Lily again, his original plan wasn't possible. Lily was the only woman he'd marry, and there was no way any relationship between them would ever be confined to a business contract.

He hadn't slept with anyone since he'd broken up with Lily, not that there hadn't been available women in Idaho. Nevertheless, on the rare Saturday nights he'd gone to town with his crew for drinks at the local bar, he'd never taken a woman home.

He might have left Lily behind in Seattle, but she'd never been out of his head, he thought. Since that first time he saw her, she'd been the only woman he'd wanted.

Cornelia was going to love her, and since Ava was very much a part of the picture, Harry should be delighted since he wouldn't have to wait a year for a grandchild.

Harry would have to agree to make Lily an exception to the rules for the Bride Hunt.

He glanced at his watch. He felt a real urgency to convince Harry to modify the terms of the contract they'd all signed. He wanted to focus all his attention on Lily and Ava.

He punched his cell phone's speed dial.

"Yes, Justin?" His assistant, as always, sounded calm, capable and unflappable.

"I need you to contact my father and brothers and tell them I have to meet with them tonight. Harry's place at…" He looked at his watch. "Ten o'clock—that should give them enough time."

"Yes, sir. And the subject of the meeting?"

"Tell them it's about the hunt."

"The hunt?"

"They'll know what I mean—and call me back to confirm."

He parked the Escalade and went upstairs to his apartment. He spent the next ninety minutes making calls, the first to his attorney to discuss changing his will to provide for Lily and Ava. When his assistant phoned to confirm he'd reached all of the Hunts and they would be at the Shack by 10:00 p.m., Justin had just finished making arrangements with his foreman to take over for him at the ranch for a few weeks. His plans to return to Idaho had been postponed indefinitely.

For the second time in a week, Justin joined his brothers in Harry's library to wait for their father.

"What are we doing here, Justin?" Gray asked. "We were all at the office yesterday, couldn't we have had this meeting then?"

"No."

"That's it? That's all you're going to give us?" J.T. eyed him. "What's going on?"

"I'll tell you as soon as Harry gets here."

"Why—" Alex began, but was interrupted when Harry entered the room.

"'Evening, boys." He joined them. "Nice to see you all again so soon. Since you said this was important, Justin, I canceled a meeting at the Redmond campus to be here." He took a seat in one of the leather armchairs and looked expectantly at his youngest son.

"I can't meet your terms for the Bride Hunt," Justin said.

The blunt words clearly surprised Harry. His brows lowered, his eyes shrewd behind his dark framed glasses as he examined him. "Why not?"

"Because last night I learned I have a daughter."

Harry sucked in an audible, startled breath. Then he beamed. "How old is she? Where is she? Who's the mother?"

"She must be about a year old, give or take a month or two." Justin ignored Harry's last two questions and addressed the issue he considered paramount. "She's mine and I mean to claim her."

"Of course," Harry said promptly. "Just as soon as you get the blood-test results."

Justin went silent. He hadn't thought about asking Lily to cooperate in paternity blood tests because it hadn't occurred to him to question whether she'd been faithful while they were dating. *Is it possible I trust her that much?* The thought stunned him.

"Well?" Harry prompted. "You did call our attorney to schedule the blood tests, didn't you? The sooner you get it done, the better."

"No." Justin shook his head. "And I won't."

Harry looked dumbfounded. "Why not? Surely

you're not going to take the mother's word as proof the child is yours?"

"That—plus she looks just like me. She's got my hair and dimples. In fact…" He narrowed his eyes at Harry. "I'd say there's a definite Hunt-family resemblance."

"That's all very well and good, but I'd venture to say a certain percentage of babies born each week have black hair and dimples. And I doubt every one of them belongs to you."

"You may be right, Harry." Justin shrugged. "But none of them have Lily for a mother."

"You're telling me you know for a fact this woman wouldn't lie to you?" Harry was clearly incredulous.

"Not about this. And before you tell me I'm crazy, Harry," Justin went on, stopping the protest he knew his father was about to make, "think about whether you'd believe Cornelia if she were the woman involved."

"Of course I would," Harry said promptly. "But she's a woman in a million."

"So is Lily. I'm not asking her for blood tests."

Harry opened his mouth, then apparently thought better of whatever he was about to say, pausing before speaking. "What about the mother?"

"What about her?"

"Are you two getting married?"

"I don't know." Justin had no intention of telling Harry he meant to marry Lily, at least not until he'd actually convinced her to do so.

"Why not?" Harry glared, clearly displeased with the news.

"She might not want to marry me."

"Of course she does. You're a Hunt."

"You know, Harry," Justin drawled, "that's not necessarily a guarantee she'll say yes."

"Why the hell not?" Harry's eyebrows lifted in surprise.

"It's…complicated." Justin didn't want to admit that if it weren't for Ava, he doubted Lily would have agreed to spend time with him. Especially since she might have good reason not to want him in her life, given the way their prior association had ended.

"Well, make it simple," Harry said bluntly.

"You've got a child. You and her mother should be married."

"Yeah, like that worked so well for you?" Justin said heatedly.

"No, it didn't work for me. Not at all. That's why Cornelia has to meet the women you pick for wives. She can spot a gold digger a mile away. In fact, she warned me not to marry every single one of your mothers."

"Great," J.D. muttered.

"If I'd listened to her," Harry went on, ignoring all of their skeptical expressions, "I wouldn't have been divorced four times."

"And none of us would be here," Gray put in, his voice dry.

"That's not my point." Harry glowered at him. "The point is that having children is a good thing, but raising children with a partner is better." He looked at Justin. "When can Cornelia and I meet your young woman?"

"You can't."

"Why not?"

"Because she doesn't want anything to do with

me at the moment and I don't want her feeling pressured by you."

"I wouldn't pressure her." Harry looked offended at the thought.

"Harry, you don't know how *not* to pressure someone. You're like a bulldozer. I don't want you going near her. *When* we work things out and *if* she wants to meet you, I'll let you know."

"Humph." Harry was clearly not satisfied with Justin's response but appeared resigned, for the moment.

"Where are the cigars, Justin?" Gray asked.

"What cigars?"

"Don't new fathers pass out cigars?"

"Oh, yeah." He grinned at his brothers. "I guess they do. I'll have to get some."

"At least we can lift a glass to the new addition to the family." Harry poured whiskey into five glasses from the decanter on the nearby table and handed one to each of his sons. "To the newest addition to our family," he said, then paused. "What's her name, Justin?"

"Ava."

"To Ava—the first little girl in our all-male family."

They saluted Justin with their glasses, tossing back the shots of aged whiskey.

Much later, Justin lay in bed, thinking about the evening's events. Harry had been surprisingly cooperative in changing the rules of the Bride Hunt for him. But then, he thought, Lily and Ava provided an instant answer to his original demands. Except for the requirement that the bride not know I'm rich, he amended. Or for Cornelia to approve my choice. He suspected Ava had a lot to do with Harry's capitulation. The old man was clearly delighted and fascinated by the existence of the girl.

Justin left his office early the next afternoon and arrived at Lily's town house at four-thirty. They repeated the previous night's routine, except this time, Ava wasn't as cooperative. She was fractious and cranky, swinging from laughter to tears within moments and refusing to eat strained carrots, usually her favorite vegetable.

"She didn't nap long enough this afternoon," Lily told Justin when the toddler refused to let him tuck her into her crib.

"You're sure that's all it is? She's not sick or something?" he asked dubiously, eyeing the sobbing little girl. Ava clung to Lily, her tears dampening the neckline of her scoop-necked T-shirt.

"I'm sure." Lily patted Ava's back, her voice soothing. "We'll rock for a few minutes and I'm guessing she'll fall asleep before I tuck her in."

"I'll wait for you downstairs." Justin didn't give Lily a chance to disagree or suggest he go on home. He switched off the lamp, leaving the room softly lit by a Winnie-the-Pooh night-light, and stepped into the hall.

He waited, listening to Lily's voice as it lifted into the first bars of a lullaby before he jogged silently down the flight of stairs. By the time Lily joined him some fifteen minutes later, he'd straightened the room, putting away scattered toys and books. He'd also tidied the kitchen, rinsing Ava's bowl and spoon and scrubbing the remains of her evening meal from her high chair's tray and seat.

"Thanks, Justin, but you don't have to do the dishes," Lily protested, her eyes widening as she glanced around the clean kitchen and neat living room.

"No problem, it's done."

"Well, thank you again. To be honest, I was dreading cleaning up. After coping with a cranky Ava today, all I really feel like doing is collapsing in front of the TV. It's very nice of you to help out, especially since I'm sure you don't do this at home," she said, hanging the damp dish towel over a drying bar.

"Sure I do," he replied. "Well, not baby dishes or high chairs," he conceded, "but I wash my dishes and pick up my clothes and boots."

"Right," she said dryly. "I seem to remember you telling me you have a full-time housekeeper at your ranch. And I know you have maid service here in Seattle."

"You're right on both counts," he admitted. "But I spent most of last year rebuilding a property

I bought to expand the ranch. The house there is old and stripped-down basic. My housekeeper would have quit if I'd asked her to leave headquarters and join us there."

"So you spent a year washing your own dishes and cleaning your own house?" Lily looked skeptical. "What about cooking?"

"The crew and I took turns in the kitchen." Justin grinned at her patent disbelief. "I haven't always been rich, you know. Until I was twelve, I pretty much took care of myself. If I hadn't learned how to cook a few basic things, I would have gone hungry."

Lily gave him a startled look.

"What?" he asked. "You don't believe I could learn to cook?"

"It's not that." She shook her head, her expression curious. "Why were you taking care of yourself until you were twelve? Where was your father or the nanny, or the housekeeper or whoever he hired to take care of you and your brothers?"

"I didn't live with Harry until I was twelve."

"I thought you'd always lived with your father."

"No, not until my grandfather died and his wife called Harry to come get me." Justin really didn't want to go into the sordid details of those early years he'd spent with his mother before she'd dumped him with her ranch-foreman father and disappeared. By the look on Lily's face, he guessed she was about to ask more questions. "It's not important who I lived with as a kid, that's ancient history," he continued before she could speak. "What *is* important is Ava. Now that I know I have a daughter, I can't walk away from her. You know that, don't you?"

She crossed her arms over her chest in a defensive gesture and stared at him for a long moment. "Aren't you going to ask for paternity test?"

"Why would I?"

"Don't you need proof you're her father?"

He shook his head, surprised she'd asked. "Lily, she looks like a combination of me and you. Unless you were dating two men with black hair and dimples two years ago, she's mine."

Tears welled in her green eyes and she brushed

them away with an irritated gesture. "Just when I'm convinced you're a jerk, you do something nice," she said, her voice trembling. "Why couldn't you have been the kind of man who'd deny paternity to keep from paying child support?"

"I'll pay child support," he said swiftly, glad she'd been the one to broach the subject. "In fact, I want to talk to my attorney about setting up a college fund for Ava. We should discuss how much you need each month and I'll have him set up an account for—"

"No." Lily held up her hand palm out, to stop him. "I don't want money from you. This isn't about money. I don't want Ava being weighed and valued in terms of dollars." Her face was flushed, her green eyes sparking with conviction.

"Neither do I," he said calmly. He'd clearly hit a nerve—and she clearly felt passionately about not taking his money. *Oh, babe, Harry and Cornelia are going to love you.*

"Which is why we *will* have those blood tests," she said firmly.

He lifted an eyebrow in surprise, studying her face. "Why?"

"Because if we don't, the question of whether she is or isn't your daughter will follow her all her life. I won't let that happen."

"All right." He paused. "Would you like me to take care of the arrangements?"

"Yes, thank you. Unless…" She frowned, thinking. "Are you sure any reporters won't hear about it?"

"I'll make sure they don't. I'll call a friend at the hospital and ask him to set it up for us."

"Good." The tension in her slim form eased. She stared at him for a moment before she shook her head, clearly puzzled. "I can't believe I'm insisting on paternity tests. I was so sure *you'd* be the one to demand proof."

"To what purpose? I'm sure she's mine." He smiled slightly, knowing his easy acceptance still baffled Lily. "Besides, I want to be part of Ava's life—although I know that might not be what you'd planned."

"None of this is what I planned." Lily waved

her arms at him. "You said goodbye to me. You told me you didn't do long-term relationships or marriage and all the things that went with it, like children. What's changed?"

"I saw Ava." *And I've never gotten you out of my head.*

"That's it? You saw her and suddenly you want to play daddy?" She was clearly unconvinced, studying him with suspicion. "That's too simple. There must be more behind your sudden switch from confirmed bachelor to dedicated father."

There isn't, but if you ever find out about Harry's Bride Hunt, you'll never believe me. The thought chilled Justin.

"Ava's mine," he said. "You're not denying I'm her father, are you?"

"Of course not," Lily shot back. "I'm just surprised that you're not more skeptical."

"We've already established I'm glad I have a daughter. I'm also a little surprised and downright stunned, maybe, but glad. I think it's time we talked about how we're going to deal with it."

She stiffened. "What do you mean?"

"I mean I want to be an active participant in her life. I want to help take care of her."

"Exactly how do you see yourself accomplishing that when your life is in Idaho and Ava is here in Seattle?" Lily asked, her tone wary.

"I'm not sure how I can make it work when I'm at the ranch. But at the moment it's not a problem since I'm here."

"For how long?"

"I'm not sure." It was too soon to tell her he wanted her to marry him so they could share Ava permanently. The suspicion in her eyes and her defensive posture warned him to move carefully. "My being in the city has other benefits—Harry's happy I'm showing up at the office in person instead of teleconferencing."

"What happens to the ranch while you're here?"

"I have a dependable crew. They've been with me for years and the foreman is reliable. He'll take over for me while I'm away."

"Oh." She walked to the sink and stood looking out the window at the minuscule backyard, her back to him.

Justin had the distinct impression she was trying to come up with a plan to convince him to return to Idaho. Not that it would work, he thought, but at least she wasn't flatly denying him access to Ava.

"My calendar's empty from ten to two tomorrow," he said. "Can I take you and Ava to lunch?"

She turned, leaning back against the cabinet. "I'm sorry but we can't—Ava has a playdate with another little girl tomorrow at eleven and I'm packing sack lunches."

"A playdate?" he said blankly. *What the hell is a playdate?*

He must have looked as confused as he felt because Lily half smiled at him, her expression easing.

"We're meeting another mother and her little girl at the Ballard Commons Park so they can play in the sprinklers. It's a good opportunity for Ava to practice interacting with other children."

"Ah, I see." He didn't, exactly, but at least now he knew a definition for *playdate*.

"Ava spends her days with adults," Lily continued. "Parenting experts agree it's important for children to have the chance to associate with other children, so she has playdates."

"Does she actually play with other kids? What do they do?"

His earliest memories of playing with other kids involved hitting a baseball; somehow he couldn't picture Ava swinging a bat.

"One-year-olds don't really play together," Lily explained. "Mostly, they play by themselves while they keep an eye on the other child. It gives them a chance to observe, though, and grow accustomed to being around other little people."

"You know a lot about being a good mother," he said. "How did you learn all this?"

"I'm sure I must have told you about my Aunt Shirley?"

Justin nodded. "She's the aunt who raised you after your parents died when you were a baby, right?"

"Yes. I wasn't sure you'd remember." Lily smiled at him, her gaze softening. "She was an amazing mother to me, although she'd never been married or had children of her own. When I called her in San Francisco to tell her I was pregnant and about how worried I was about being a good mom, she convinced me I'd muddle through. And she was right—somehow I've managed to do this for a whole year," she laughed, her posture relaxed. "Mostly through trial and error. Plus there are literally hundreds of books available for new mothers, filled with great information."

"I can see I'll have to start reading, I've got a lot to catch up on. I'm assuming there are books for fathers, too?"

"Yes." Her gaze met his, warm with shared understanding for a brief moment. Then she appeared to realize she'd dropped the barriers between them and she looked at her watch. "Well, um…it's getting late. I still have work to do tonight."

"I'll take off." He left the kitchen area and she followed him to the foyer. "Would you mind if I dropped by the park tomorrow?"

Her mouth tightened and he was sure she was

going to refuse. But then she seemed to rethink and reluctantly nodded. "I'm sure Ava would be happy to see you."

"Then I'll see you both tomorrow." He pulled open the door and paused, looking down at her. A curl lay against her cheek, and without thinking, he brushed it back, tucking the silky hair behind her ear.

Lily instantly ducked away from his hand. "Don't."

"Don't?" Justin echoed, shoving his fingertips into his jeans pockets to keep from reaching for her. Only a moment earlier, she'd let him touch her cheek and hair, but now instinct told him she'd only move farther away if he did what his body urged him to do and tried to pull her close.

Those brief moments of ease between them as they discussed Ava were gone, and she was once again barricaded behind thick emotional walls. He couldn't blame her. He knew she had good reasons not to trust him, but her rejections, coming on the heels of those earlier warm moments, made his heart ache.

She folded her arms across her chest, hugging herself defensively. "I want to be perfectly clear, Justin, none of this is about us. There is no 'us.' You're here in my house because you're Ava's father. We have no other connection."

"No?" His voice rumbled, deep and gravelly. "Are you sure about that?"

"Absolutely." Her chin firmed with stubbornness.

"If you say so," he said, his voice neutral. If she wanted to believe that, fine. He knew damn well there was a lot of something between them, but she seemed determined to deny the heat that arced between them, and for some reason, he didn't want to force the issue. Maybe it was because he didn't want to jeopardize the truce they'd called for Ava's sake; maybe it was because he felt badly because of the way their earlier relationship had ended. Or maybe it was because she looked so damned wary, as if she'd run if he made a move toward her. Whatever it was, he wasn't willing to rock the boat and risk scaring her off.

"So…" His voice rasped and he cleared his throat. "I'll see you and Ava tomorrow, then."

She nodded without speaking and he jogged down her front steps, hearing the door close behind him with a decisive click.

I've got a lot of damage to undo before I suggest we get married for Ava's sake, he realized. *I have to convince her to trust me again.*

He only wished he knew how the hell he was going to do that.

Chapter Four

The Ballard Commons Park was semi-busy a half hour before lunch. Mothers occupied the benches and watched their children playing in the small, knee-high geysers of water erupting from the ground-level sprinklers in the concrete pad. On the far side of the concrete area, several older boys and girls rode skateboards back and forth.

"Wow, is that your guy?"

Lily looked up from adjusting Ava's damp bathing suit. Seated on the bench beside her, Chris focused her gaze on the street to their left, her eyes wide.

Lily half turned to look over her shoulder. Her heart stuttered as she caught sight of Justin walking across the strip of grass separating the sidewalk and street from the sprinkler area. He wore cowboy boots, faded Levi's and a white T-shirt with a small ranch logo over his upper left chest. The white cotton stretched over his biceps, his muscled arms tanned and powerful. She couldn't see his eyes behind his Ray-Ban sunglasses, but she could feel the intensity of his gaze as he strode toward them.

"Um, yes. That's him," she managed to say when she realized Chris was staring at her.

"Sooo," Chris said, amusement and curiosity on her face as she handed a cracker to her two-year-old daughter, Amanda. "You didn't tell me you two are an item."

"We're not an item," Lily denied vehemently before remembering she definitely didn't want to confess that the reason she was seeing Justin was because he was Ava's father. "I mean, not exactly."

"Of course you're not," Chris said with patent disbelief. Amanda tugged on her sleeve and Chris popped an apple slice into the little girl's mouth, laughing with the toddler when the juice ran down her chin.

Lily would have made a further denial but Justin reached the bench where they sat.

"Good morning, Lily." He smiled at her, Chris and Amanda, then tickled Ava under her chin. "Hey, peanut, how's my girl?"

Ava giggled, squirmed and babbled back at him before she held out both arms. He looked ridiculously pleased and surprised before he shot a quick, questioning look at Lily. When she nodded her permission, he slipped his hands around Ava's waist and picked her up, cradling her awkwardly against his chest.

She responded by chortling and patting his face with her hands before she reached for his Ray-Bans.

"Hey, wait a minute," he protested, laughing as he juggled her closer and caught one of her tiny hands in his.

"Don't let her take your glasses," Lily warned.

"Everything goes in her mouth and she'll chew on them. And very likely break them, too."

"Uh-oh." Justin shifted the glasses atop his head with one hand, his eyes crinkling at the corners as he smiled at Ava. He brushed his hand over her curls. "Hey, you're damp." He looked at Lily. "Has she been in the water already?"

"Yes, she loves it."

"Mind if I take her again?"

"Not at all, go ahead."

"If you'll hold her, I'll take off my boots." He handed Ava back to Lily and sat down next to her on the end of the bench.

Chris nudged Lily and waggled her eyebrows, looking significantly at Justin.

"Justin, I'd like you to meet my friend, Chris, and her daughter, Amanda. Chris, this is Justin. He lives in Idaho," she added pointedly.

"That would explain the cowboy boots," Chris commented with a grin. "Hi, Justin."

"Hi, Chris. Nice to meet you." Justin smiled at Chris, gave Lily a swift, narrow-eyed glance and leaned forward to pull off his boots.

"How long are you going to be here in Seattle?" Chris asked.

"Indefinitely." Justin stuffed his socks into his boots, shoved them under the bench and stood. He took Ava from Lily. "Certainly weeks, maybe for months, maybe longer."

Lily stared at him, taken aback. He was kidding, wasn't he?

He smiled at her and winked, dimples appearing in his cheeks, before he strolled off, carrying on a murmured conversation with Ava.

"Be still my heart." Chris pressed her palm to her chest. She sounded faintly breathless. "He even has dimples. He's gorgeous. Why haven't you told me about him?" she demanded, her expression curious and speculative as she looked from Justin to Lily.

"There's nothing to tell," Lily protested. "He's an acquaintance who's visiting in town and I've seen him a few times over the last week, that's all."

"He doesn't look at you as if you two are 'just friends.' I'm guessing there's a lot more to this than you're telling me, especially since he looks just like Ava," Chris said. "But, hey, if you don't want to share info…" Her voice trailed off, her expression hopeful.

Lily pretended not to hear the invitation in Chris's voice to confide details about Justin. She wasn't ready to tell anyone Justin was Ava's father, especially since she was fairly certain it wouldn't be long before Chris discovered Justin's identity as Harrison Hunt's son.

"Mommy." Amanda tugged on Chris's hand. "Let's play."

"Okay, hon." Chris stood. "Ready to get wet again, Lily?"

"Thanks, I think I'll pass." Lily stretched out her legs, bare and still damp beneath the hem of her short full skirt, as Chris and Amanda walked away, hand in hand.

Justin and Ava were on the far side of the bank of spinklers. His jeans were spattered with water from his knees to the hems. He held Ava's hand as she walked, sometimes staggering uncertainly, sometimes wobbling, but always with a determination that was palpable.

The sun gleamed on their heads, their hair identical shades of coal-black. Ava giggled as she reached for a jet of water and it sprayed her face. She looked up at Justin, dimples denting her round baby cheeks as he laughed down at her, and Lily's heart wrenched.

They look so much alike, she realized. Daddy and daughter at play. If Chris hadn't guessed already, she soon would.

She felt her resolve to keep her heart frozen and Justin at arm's length weakening as she watched him swing Ava up and brush water drops from her cheeks.

Bouquets of summer flowers from the Gazebo were arriving on her doorstep every day, but the gifts didn't change her feelings toward Justin.

The laughter on Ava's face as Justin swung her in a circle and then lowered her toward the small jet of water, however, threatened to put a huge dent in her belief that he was strictly bad news.

An hour later, Lily waved goodbye as Chris and Amanda pulled away from the park, relieved that her friend apparently hadn't identified Justin.

Still, it was only a matter of time. Lily had to wonder how long before some newspaper reporter spotted Justin with Ava and put two and two together.

She hoped that day was far in the future. She wasn't ready to field questions about Justin's place in her and Ava's life.

"There we go." Justin snapped the latch on Ava's car seat, kissed her cheek and stepped back, closing the door. "I have to fly to Portland overnight on business, but I'll be back tomorrow afternoon," he said as he turned to Lily. "Are you okay with me dropping by to help you with Ava after work?"

"I'm sorry," she said. "We can't tomorrow night. I have a date." She hadn't meant to tell him quite that bluntly, but on the other hand, she was determined not to feel guilty over this. Besides, it was a charity fund-raiser and the man she was going with was a business connection—a lingerie buyer for a string of boutiques located in cities along the Pacific Coast from Seattle to San Diego.

"A date," Justin said flatly. He stared at her, his eyes narrowing. The easygoing charm disappeared and he looked suddenly dangerous. "Who's watching Ava while you're out?"

"My next-door neighbor, Mrs. Baker."

"Cancel her. I'll stay with Ava."

Startled, she felt her eyes widen in alarm. She hadn't expected this. "I booked Mrs. Baker weeks ago, Justin. I can't cancel at the last minute— she's retired and baby-sits to supplement her social security income."

"I'll pay her whatever her usual rate is, plus a bonus for the late-cancellation." His mouth tightened, a muscle flexing along his jawline. "Unless you don't trust me to take care of Ava."

"No," she denied hastily. "It's not that. I know you'd take good care of her, but…"

"Good," he interrupted. "Then we're set. What time shall I be at the house?"

"Around eight."

"See you then."

He strode away toward his vehicle. Lily climbed behind the wheel of her car, still not sure exactly what had happened. She'd expected he wouldn't be pleased when he learned she was going out.

Despite her denial there was anything between them beyond their mutual love for Ava, she had to constantly resist the sexual attraction that pulsed between them. She was fairly sure he felt it, too.

She hadn't anticipated he would offer to baby-sit while she was out. She truly didn't have any qualms about leaving Ava in his care. He adored her and was fully capable of caring for her, especially since she'd have her cell phone with her at all times and he could call if he had any questions. No, it was herself she wasn't sure about. She felt oddly as if she was betraying him by going out on a date with someone else.

She frowned and got into the car, slamming the door closed.

I have no reason whatsoever to feel guilty.

Yet she did.

It was extremely annoying. And disconcerting since there was no reason she should feel any loyalty to Justin.

The next evening, Justin knocked on Lily's door at 7:45. He thought he'd wrestled his anger into submission, but when she answered his knock, outrage roared back to life. Which I've got no right to feel since she's not mine, at least not yet, he told himself.

"Hello." She wore a little black dress with a scoop neck and tiny sleeves. The hem reached her knees, but the slim skirt had a slit up one side that flashed several inches of pale thigh when she stepped back, holding the door open.

"Hi." He walked past her and into the house, his nostrils flaring as he caught the subtle scent of her perfume. Swallowing a growl, he waited for her to close the door and move ahead of him.

"Is Ava asleep?" he asked as he followed Lily into the kitchen area.

She glanced over her shoulder. "Yes. I'm afraid she's catching a summer cold. She's been cranky and sneezing all day and didn't eat all her dinner. I gave her children's aspirin before I put her to bed." She stopped at the counter and picked up a pen, writing on a sheet of paper. "I'm jotting down the pediatrician's after-hours number and my cell phone number." She scanned the note before handing it to him. "The Pink Ladies

Society dinner is being held in the Oasis Room at the Sheraton downtown—I gave you that number, too, just in case my cell phone isn't reachable inside the hotel. If you have any questions or if Ava wakes and you can't get her back to sleep, please call me. I'll come home right away."

"Does she have a fever?" Justin scanned the list of numbers.

"She didn't have one before I put her to bed." Lily bit her lip, clearly torn. "Maybe I should cancel tonight. I've never been away from Ava when she wasn't feeling well."

Much as Justin didn't want Lily going out with some other guy, neither did he want her to stay home when she was dressed for an evening out. Besides, the function she was attending was a fund-raising benefit for Virginia Mason Hospital. He recognized the name of the event because he'd declined an invitation and sent a donation the week before. Maybe this evening was a business function and not a real date. He didn't know and he damned sure wasn't going to ask, but something inside him urged him to soothe Lily's nerves and reassure her.

"If she wakes and I have any problems, I'll call you immediately," he promised. "You shouldn't cancel your plans because our little girl has the sniffles."

"She can be very high-maintenance when she doesn't feel well," Lily warned, clearly worried.

"So can you," he said. "Remember the weekend we spent in your apartment when you caught a cold? I fed you chicken soup and we watched a marathon of classic movies?"

Her eyes darkened and a faint rose tinted her cheeks. "Yes, I remember," she murmured, her voice soft.

The doorbell rang, ending the charged moment.

"Oh, for heaven's sake," she said with annoyance. "I told Doug not to ring the doorbell. He'll wake Ava." She grabbed her purse and hurried out of the room.

Justin followed, standing behind her when she pulled open the door.

"Doug—hi."

"Hi, Lily." The lanky man on the porch swept her with one all-encompassing glance, appreciation gleaming in his dark eyes. "You look great."

"Thanks. I'd ask you in, but we're running late so we should probably go. Justin…" She looked over her shoulder and jumped slightly when her arm brushed his shirtsleeve, because he stood within touching distance. "Please call me if Ava wakes and seems worse, especially if she's running a temperature."

"I will." Justin tucked a wayward tendril behind her ear, his fingers brushing the curve of her jawline. She started, her eyes flaring in surprise. He looked away from her and met the other man's eyes with a hard stare. "You kids have fun now. And drive carefully."

Doug's expression went from surprise at the possessive gesture when Justin's hand touched Lily's hair to speculation. His hand cupped Lily's elbow and drew her over the threshold onto the porch beside him.

"Don't wait up," he said, his voice bordering on hostile.

Justin's smile bared his teeth. Fortunately, he kept from snarling. Just barely. "Oh, I'll be here when you get back," he said, his voice dangerously soft.

"Call me if Ava runs a temp," Lily said, giving him a threatening, you're-so-going-to-pay-for-this look.

He nodded and leaned against the doorjamb, watching as Doug handed Lily into a sleek BMW and they drove away.

He went inside, restraining the urge to slam the door because he didn't want to wake Ava.

Inside the car, Lily drew a deep breath.

"What was that all about?" Doug asked, downshifting the roadster as they slowed for a stop sign. "Who was that guy?"

"Justin? He's the baby-sitter—he's watching Ava tonight."

"That's not all he's watching," Doug commented. He glanced at her. "You're not married, are you, Lily?"

She stared at him, affronted. "Of course I'm

not married—I wouldn't be going out with you if I were."

"You might want to tell your baby-sitter that," Doug said. "Because he's making noises like a husband."

"I'm sure you're mistaken," Lily managed to say calmly even as her fingers squeezed her small evening purse until they left dents in the smooth black satin. "He offered to stay with Ava tonight. She adores him and he's very good with her, but that's all there is to it." Privately, Lily agreed with Doug. Justin *was* acting as if she belonged to him. She'd have to talk to him as soon as she got home. She knew him too well. If she gave him an inch, he'd take a mile, and she wasn't getting involved with him again.

The only connection possible for them was their mutual love for Ava, she told herself firmly. End of story.

The evening was a complete success—from a business standpoint. Lily made several new contacts, reconnected with a number of current clients and visited with friends in the industry. On a personal level, however, the dinner hour, followed by dancing, wasn't so successful. Doug worked the crowd with ease, which meant he spent far more time away from her side than with her. Oddly enough, Lily didn't mind. He'd been asking her out for months and she'd finally agreed, thinking the business function would be a good testing ground for whether she should say yes to a regular dinner-and-movie date.

She had her answer before the evening was over. When he drove her home and parked outside her town house, she suspected he knew what she was going to say.

"Thanks for tonight, Doug." She released her seat belt and turned to look at him. "It was fun."

"It was an extension of our workday, only in better clothes," he said wryly. "And with better food, at least for me. I'm glad you enjoyed yourself—but I'm guessing tonight was a one-time-only deal."

"I'm sorry, Doug, my life is…complicated at the moment."

"Yeah, I noticed. All six feet of him," he said, giving her a small smile.

"You're being a good sport about this," she said softly, grateful he was taking rejection so well.

"I wouldn't be if I thought I had a chance with you, but something tells me I'm going to have to settle for coworker status."

"My work life is in far better shape than my personal life at the moment, Doug, so you're getting the best of the two, trust me."

He laughed and pushed open his door. As he rounded the hood of the roadster, the light over the town house door switched on.

Doug handed Lily out of the car. He kept her hand enclosed in his and bent forward. "Do you want me to come in with you? I'd be glad to explain to your baby-sitter that we're just friends," he murmured in her ear.

"No, thanks. I appreciate the offer, but I'm good."

Doug brushed his lips against her cheek in a light kiss and stepped back, releasing her. "I'll wait here until you're inside," he told her.

"Spoken like a true gentleman, Doug."

He grinned ruefully. "You've got my number.

Call me if you ever change your mind about wanting more than a business relationship."

She laughed and walked away from him up the sidewalk, turning to wave when she reached the porch. He lifted a hand in reply, and as she climbed the steps, she heard the car's engine turn over. Just as she reached the top step and crossed the porch, Justin stepped outside.

"How's Ava?" she whispered as she entered, turning to look at him as he followed and locked the door behind them.

"She was awake earlier, but she's sleeping now."

Relief washed over Lily. "And her temperature? Did she have a fever when she woke?"

"No, but her pajamas were damp so I changed her. Then I gave her some water, we sang and walked the floor awhile, and she went back to sleep." He glanced at his watch. "That was about an hour ago. She hasn't stirred since."

"Thank goodness." She looked up at him and frowned. "We need to talk. Come into the family room so we don't wake Ava."

The lights in the kitchen area were turned off.

Only the lamp on the sofa table and the television glowed, casting fitful shadows into the far corners of the room.

Lily was too intent on confronting Justin to register the intimacy fostered by the gentle glow. She walked farther into the room, dropped her purse on the ottoman and turned to face him.

He leaned against the doorjamb, watching her with an inscrutable expression.

"What was that about—earlier?" she demanded.

"What?"

"The way you acted when Doug picked me up."

"Oh. That."

"Yes, that." She crossed her arms and glared at him. "He actually asked me if I was married—because you were acting like a husband."

"Did he?" Justin shoved away from the door frame and prowled toward her.

"Yes. And he's right about one thing—you were being territorial." She refused to back away from him. He kept coming until only inches separated them and she had to tilt her head back to look up at him. "You have no right to suggest that there's something between us. Except for Ava, we aren't connected. We aren't even casually dating. We aren't…anything."

"We aren't dating," he agreed, his voice so gravelly Lily barely understood him. "But we are definitely something."

Before she could utter a denial, his arms slipped around her and he yanked her tight against him. His mouth took hers.

Lily instinctively struggled against the intensity of the unleashed passion in his kiss. She gripped his biceps, pushing him away.

For a moment, she was afraid he was too out of control to respond, but then he froze, his muscles going rock-hard beneath her hands. She felt the tension in his body as he seemed to struggle to rein in raging emotions before his hold eased and he lifted his head.

"Lily—I'm sorry. I didn't mean to scare you." The muttered words were barely intelligible.

No longer restrained, she was swamped by sensory overload, surrounded by powerful arms that cradled her against his chest, the long muscles of his thighs rock-hard against hers. She caught her breath in an attempt to shore up her defenses, but instead drew in the scent of subtle aftershave and pure male that was unique to him.

"Justin," she breathed, aching. *I've missed you—missed this.*

Need swamped caution and her hands left his biceps and reached for him, her arms slipping around his neck as she went up on her toes. Her lips touched his and he groaned, wrapping her closer. His lips seduced hers, setting off a firestorm of heat that had her heart pounding and temperature skyrocketing.

A very small section of her brain was still capable of sanity, and allowed her to summon the strength to pull away from him at last. "This isn't going to happen," she said, her voice husky with emotion and arousal. "I'm not going there again with you."

"Too late. We're already there." His voice was raspy with arousal and conviction.

"No, it's not too late," she said fiercely, shaking her head in denial.

His arms loosened, his hands resting on her

waist as she swayed, disoriented, before she found her footing and stepped away from him.

"I want you to leave."

He stared at her silently, frustration evident in the taut line of his jaw. "I'll go," he said, his voice a rough murmur. "But let's be straight about this—whether you're ready to accept it or not, there's still something between us. And it's a lot more than nothing." He turned and strode away from her, halting at the doorway to look back at her. "I'll be back to see you—and Ava—tomorrow."

He left and she waited, arrow-straight and immobile, until the soft sound of the front door closing behind him reached her.

Then she wilted, her shoulders sagging as she lowered herself unsteadily onto the nearby sofa.

I won't fall for him again. I won't. She wrapped her arms around her midriff, her body trembling.

The potential for heartbreak was all too real. She wasn't sure she'd survive if he walked away from her again.

And he would. She was convinced of it. Despite his obvious absorption with Ava at the moment, she was sure he'd grow tired of the novelty of being a father, and when the reality of day-to-day life with a toddler sank in, he'd be gone. Maybe he'd send cards on her birthdays, maybe he'd help with college bills, but Lily couldn't imagine Justin would sign on for being more than an occasional presence in his daughter's life. He lived in Idaho most of the time, and even if he visited in Seattle, how long could he take time away from the ranch to spend hours with Ava?

I just have to get through this initial honeymoon stage he's in with Ava, she told herself. Then life will return to normal.

She stood and headed upstairs to her bed. Somewhere deep within, a small voice wondered if maybe, just maybe, this time, Justin wouldn't leave.

Chapter Five

Justin called himself seven kinds of fool as he drove away from Lily's town house.

I shouldn't have pushed her, he thought. I should have been understanding.

But knowing she'd spent the evening with another man had wiped out every civilized instinct he had. Some primal need to mark her as his had compelled him to kiss her and replace the other guy's touch with his.

He knew he wasn't being reasonable, but the

knowledge didn't seem to help his reaction to the thought of Lily allowing another man close enough to touch.

He dragged his hand down his face.

What the hell's going on with me?

He'd stayed away from Lily for two years. Now he wondered if he'd only put all his emotions on hold when he'd left her and they'd been dammed up, ready to spring free when seeing her with Ava opened the floodgates.

Whatever the answer was, he didn't see himself going back to the numbed-out state he'd been in over the past months. Not with Lily and Ava back in his life.

He had to find a way to handle this before he ruined any chance he had of convincing Lily to marry him.

Lily bent over her worktable, studying the sketches spread out over the surface. She was alone in the large open space, one floor above the boutique, and had been for the past half hour when her two assistants walked Ava across the hall to her playroom for midmorning snack. Their muted laughter carried clearly down the short hall and in through the open door.

"I just can't decide," Lily murmured to herself, shifting and reordering the sketches. When she still couldn't narrow her choices to three, she picked up her cell phone. "Meggie? Can you come upstairs? I need you to look at something for me and give me a fresh opinion."

A moment later, she heard footsteps in the hallway outside.

"Meggie," she said, still assessing the ten sketches on the tabletop. "Will you look at these and tell me which one you like best? They're the preliminary designs for the bustier samples we're making for the Standish boutique in Portland— did you have a favorite?"

"Meggie stopped across the hall to see Ava."

Lily started, taken by surprise at the deep male voice that was too familiar. She looked over her shoulder and found Justin walking toward her, his long strides quickly erasing the distance between them.

"I came by to apologize." He held out one of the two cups he carried. "And I brought you a gift—not that I think a latte will make up for how I acted last night, but I needed the caffeine and thought maybe you could use some, too."

"Thanks." Lily took the cup, torn between wanting to talk to him and a reluctance to deal with the emotions of last night.

"I was out of line and I'm sorry," he said without preamble. "Not for kissing you—I doubt I'll ever be sorry for that, even if you're mad as hell. But when you left to go out, I should have been…more polite…to your date." He said the last words reluctantly.

Lily eyed him over the rim of her cup. "As apologies go, this isn't the most sincere one I've ever heard."

He ran his hand over his hair, rumpling it, and scowled. "I know. I'm trying to do the right thing, but the truth is, I suspect I'll probably be just as bad if I ever have to live through a repeat of last night."

"Are you telling me I can't go out with other

men?" Lily demanded, hackles rising. Not that she wanted to, she told herself, but he didn't know that.

"No." He shook his head. "I'm not. Of course I'm not. I don't have the right…"

"Good. I'm glad we agree."

"…but if you could postpone dating until we figured out this thing with you, me and Ava, I'd appreciate it."

She frowned, unsure exactly what he meant. "I thought we were doing fairly well with the situation—you're spending time with Ava and she's getting to know you. What else is there?"

"Maybe that's all there would be for two other people in this situation—but there's more between us than Ava. I still have…feelings for you." His voice was rougher, deeper, his gaze intense. "And I don't think you're immune to me. Maybe all you feel is anger because I wasn't around when you found out you were pregnant, or maybe you resent me because I broke off with you two years ago. I can't say for sure what's going on here, but I'm damned sure this isn't only about our child. And if you're honest, Lily, I think you'll agree."

Lily badly wanted to deny she had any feelings for him beyond what she felt for any other man she'd dated. But she wasn't good at lying, and even if she were, she doubted he'd believe her.

"Maybe there is something," Lily said carefully. "But as you say, any emotion on my part may well come from anger. I won't deny there were times when I thought I hated you after you left and I learned I was pregnant. Whether that's all there is, I don't know."

He drew a deep breath and slowly exhaled. "Okay, that's fair," he said as he nodded, absently rubbing his palm over his chest, just above his heart. "I can work with that. Will you do me a favor?"

"What?" She was almost afraid to hear what he wanted. If he asked her to be more specific, she wasn't sure she could without lying.

"I know I made mistakes with you and I have a lot to make up for. I'm going to convince you that you can trust me again."

He looked around, sweeping her workspace with an assessing eye. "Great place you've got— it seems bigger than the last time I was here. How many employees do you have now?"

Relieved their conversation about feelings was apparently finished, Lily showed him around the open-space workroom before they went across the hall to see Ava.

"I have to fly to Idaho on business this afternoon," Justin said as he kissed Ava's cheek and handed her to Lily an hour later. "I might be gone a couple of days, but I'll be back by Monday at the latest."

"Then we'll see you when you return." Lily ignored the sudden disappointment and purposely made her smile brighter.

He leaned forward and brushed a kiss against her cheek, then her mouth. "Miss me," he murmured into her ear, the words a soft command.

Before she could protest, he turned and disappeared down the stairs. She heard his deep tones as he made a comment, followed by Meggie's laughter, then the bells on the outer door jingled.

Lily carried Ava into her playroom, the feel of his warm mouth against hers lingering long after he was gone.

The small neighborhood park around the corner from their town house was a favorite with Lily and Ava. On Saturday morning, she held Ava on her lap while they sat in one of the swings, moving slowly back and forth while Ava giggled with delight. Afterward, they strolled over the expanse of lawn, Ava clutching Lily's finger while she practiced walking, lurching along with frequent sudden falls onto her diaper-padded bottom. When she tired of the exercise, Lily fed her a picnic lunch sitting cross-legged on a light quilt spread on the thick grass. Ava fell asleep after eating. She lay sprawled on her back on the cotton quilt, her favorite blankie tucked over her with the soft pink ribbon edging clutched tightly in one hand.

Lily sat on the quilt beside Ava, knees raised, her bare toes flexing in the cool grass at the edge of the cotton spread. She opened her book, a romance by her favorite author, Susan Wiggs, but instead of reading, she stared unseeingly at the far edge of the park.

What am I going to do about Justin?

He was being attentive, considerate, charming, and clearly adored Ava. So why was she so unsettled and worried about his sudden reappearance?

The answer was obvious, but it wasn't one Lily wanted to acknowledge.

He still had the power to wreck her life, she thought. All he had to do was walk into a room and her inner radar shivered and cranked on high-alert. Her stupid hormones still went haywire every time he got close enough to let her breathe in that unique scent of subtle aftershave and pure male that was his alone.

The necessity of balancing his legal and moral right to see Ava with her own need to keep him as far away as possible was driving her crazy. She badly wanted to tell him to go away, but not only would it be a poor decision, as her attorney had assured her only yesterday, but Ava clearly adored him.

Ugh. She dropped her head into her hands and

groaned silently. *I should never have left the flower shop with him that night all those months ago.*

But then you wouldn't have Ava. The small voice spoke clearly and with indisputable logic.

Lily lifted her head and looked at her daughter. Ava was sound asleep, her long dark lashes delicate fans against smooth skin, her compact little body sprawled with the boneless ease of childhood slumber. A surge of love rocked Lily, calming the storm of emotions stirred by thoughts of Justin.

You're worth it, Ava, she thought. You're the best thing that's ever happened to me.

Calmer, she returned to her novel, this time totally absorbed in the pages.

"Hello."

Lily looked up from her book. An older man in a white golf shirt, khaki pants and brown loafers had taken a seat on the nearby park bench. A blue Mariners baseball cap covered most of his black hair and his eyes were concealed behind dark sunglasses. He nodded, smiling in friendly greeting.

She smiled back and he shook out his newspaper and began to read.

The man looked familiar, she thought as she bent her head to her novel once more.

"Humph, what nonsense," the man grumbled.

"I beg your pardon?" Lily looked up, unsure if he were talking to her, or commenting to himself.

"Sorry." The man lowered his newspaper and shook his head with a faint grimace. "Politics—drives me crazy."

Lily smiled. "Me, too. What's the city council up to now?"

"Potholes," he said succinctly. "They don't see the need to fill the ones on streets in the SoDo District."

"SoDo, specifically?" Lily suspected the pothole issue applied to more city streets than just those in SoDo, local shorthand for the Seattle area located "south-of-downtown." "I've noticed a few problems in Fremont, too."

"This report is about the Sodo District in particular." He held up the paper, turning it so she could see the photo of the mayor talking to a road crew. Two of the four men were shoveling black, grainy-looking material into a hole the size of a large bucket. "I drive down there, past Safeco Field, several times a week, and believe me, the streets are in terrible shape in the warehouse area."

"As much as we pay in taxes, you'd think the city could afford to fill potholes before they're so big a car could fall into them," Lily said dryly.

The man's eyebrows lifted and he laughed, an abrupt bark of sound.

Beside Lily, Ava stirred, murmuring and curling onto her side.

"I'm sorry," the man said, his gruff voice lower, quieter. "I didn't mean to wake her."

Lily stroked her palm lightly over Ava's back, feeling her settle once more. "It's okay, she's still sleeping."

"How old is she?" he asked.

"A year." Lily glanced at him, and was surprised at his strangely vulnerable expression as he stared at Ava. The newspaper twitched as if stirred by a breeze, but the day was still. "Do you have grandchildren?"

"Yes."

"Girls or boys?"

"A little girl." His gaze left Ava's tiny form and met hers. "A brand-new little granddaughter. I wasn't sure I'd have grandchildren," he went on, his deep voice faintly rough. "I didn't set a good example as a father, or as a husband. I wasn't sure any of my kids would want to marry, let alone have children."

"Then you must be even more delighted to finally have a granddaughter," Lily said, caught by the emotion in his voice.

"I am," he said with quiet conviction. "I truly am." He looked at Ava, then returned to Lily. "Are you and your husband planning more children?"

"I don't think so," Lily said cautiously. The man seemed nice, but she wasn't sure she wanted to share personal details about her life with a stranger.

"Well, if you do," the man said with a smile, "I hope they're all as beautiful as your little girl there." He pointed to Ava before glancing at his watch. "Uh-oh, where did the time go? I'm going to be late." He folded his paper and stood. "Nice talking to you." He lifted a hand in farewell before striding briskly away down the walkway.

Lily watched him leave, struck by how tall he was—he had to be well over six feet, she thought. The nagging feeling that she knew him returned, stronger than before. Was he a customer at the boutique? No, not likely, she thought, although there were a number of male regulars who bought lingerie for their wives. Most of her clientele, however, were women.

A black SUV pulled up to the curb, the door was pushed open by an invisible someone in the back seat and the man got in, then the vehicle quickly sped away.

Beside her, Ava stirred, waking from her nap and distracting Lily. It wasn't until later that afternoon as she scanned the daily online version of the *Seattle Post-Intelligencer* that she realized the man in the park had been none other than Harrison Hunt.

She stared at the picture in disbelief, narrowing her eyes to focus.

The photograph had been taken at a charity

function months earlier and Harrison wore a
tuxedo. Black-rimmed glasses framed his shrewd
gaze and his black hair was uncovered, but
nevertheless, Lily was positive the man in the
photo and the man she'd spoken with in the park
earlier were one and the same. The casual clothes,
dark sunglasses and the Mariners ball cap he'd
worn, plus the fact that a small neighborhood park
in Ballard was the last place she would have
expected to see the billionaire, had created near-
perfect camouflage.

She thought about their conversation and
realized there could only be one reason Harry had
sought her out—Justin must have told him about
Ava. And Harrison apparently had wanted a closer
look at his granddaughter.

Why didn't he introduce himself? she wondered.
In retrospect, he'd seemed almost shaken as he
studied Ava, the newspaper trembling in his hands.

Lily hadn't worried when the older gentleman
in the park was an unknown. But now that she
knew he was Harrison Hunt, her protective instincts went on red alert. She didn't know Harry

personally—Justin hadn't introduced her to anyone in his family when they were dating. Nevertheless, she'd read accounts of Harry's brilliant deal making and ruthlessly competitive business nature.

What was the likelihood Harrison Hunt was a sweet teddy bear in his personal dealings?

I'm guessing it's zero to none.

So what did that say about why he'd come looking for Ava today? She glanced at the digital clock on the microwave in the corner cabinet. Only a few hours until Justin was due to arrive, and when he did, she thought, he'd better have an explanation for his father's unexpected visit to Ballard.

She waited until Ava was tucked into bed and they were downstairs again, the brightly lit family room allowing her to see his expressions clearly and judge his reactions.

"I talked to your father today."

Justin's head came up and he stared at her. "What?"

"I saw Harry today," she repeated.

"Where?"

"At the park. Ava and I spent a couple of hours there this morning, and after we ate lunch, your father arrived."

"What did he want?"

"He sat down on a bench nearby and he read the newspaper. Then we talked about how much we both don't like politics in general and the city's failure to fill in street potholes in particular. Then he asked me how old Ava was—and, that's about it."

"That's it? What did you say when he told you who he was?"

"He didn't tell me who he was."

Justin's eyes narrowed at her, trying to gauge her mood. "He never identified himself?"

She shook her head. "No. I didn't realize who he was until after we were home and I saw a photo of him online."

"So you don't know what he wanted?"

"I thought maybe you could tell me."

"I told him to stay away from you until you were ready to meet him, whenever that might be." *What the hell was Harry up to?* "He didn't say anything that gave you an indication as to why he was there?"

"I think he did, although I didn't realize it at the time. He talked about wanting grandchildren and he told me he had a new granddaughter."

Justin bit back a curse.

"He was talking about Ava, wasn't he?" Lily went on when he didn't speak. "You told him about Ava?"

"Yeah, I told him I—we—have a daughter," Justin admitted, wondering how much he should tell her. "Harry suffered a heart attack recently, and ever since, he's been fixated on the fact that none of his sons are married with kids."

"Oh, yes," Lily said. "He mentioned he'd been concerned that none of his sons had children. I didn't know at the time you were one of the 'sons' he was talking about," she added. "But then, I didn't know he was Harrison Hunt."

"Harry's pretty hard to miss—especially given all the high-profile interviews he does for HuntCom. Why didn't you recognize him?" Justin asked, curious.

Lily shrugged. "He looked like any other over-sixty guy in the park. And he was dressed down, in khakis and a golf shirt, with dark sunglasses and a ball cap."

"Harry was wearing a ball cap?" Justin was incredulous.

"Yes—a blue-and-gold Mariners hat." She eyed him. "You look shocked."

"I am." Justin shook his head, amazed. "Harry considered buying the team once, but even if he had, I doubt he would have worn the hat. He's just not a casual-clothes kind of guy."

"Well, he was today," Lily said dryly. "And the hat and glasses made a very effective disguise. Besides, who would have expected a billionaire to drop into my little neighborhood park on a Saturday morning to read his paper?"

"You've got a point." Justin was relieved. Lily wasn't giving off hostile vibes. Apparently, Harry hadn't said anything to offend her. "So, you're okay with him dropping in on you?"

She bit her lip, her eyes going dark green. "I'm concerned about why he did it. If he only wanted to meet Ava, why didn't he call and ask to see her? Why didn't he tell me who he was at the park?"

"Maybe because I warned him not to contact you," Justin said. "Harry on a mission can be hard to deal with. I didn't want him pressuring you in any way."

"What kind of pressure did you think he might use?" she asked.

Justin could tell his words hadn't reassured her, in fact, just the opposite. She looked alarmed. "Nothing specific," he said soothingly. "It's just Harry's personality to get intense about things. I didn't want you to feel overwhelmed by him. Or by the rest of my family," he added. "My brothers are cool with waiting to meet you until you're ready, but the women in the family are as excited about Ava as Harry. I had a message on my answering machine from my aunt Cornelia, and another one from my cousin Frankie."

"What did you tell them?" Lily asked.

"Nothing. I haven't called them back. But when I do," he added, seeing the tiny frown lines deepen between her brows. "I'll tell them to back off until you say it's time. Okay?"

"Okay." She smiled, clearly relieved. "Thanks,

Justin. It's not that I don't want to meet them, and I'm sure my Aunt Shirley wants to meet you, too. But I know the press keeps track of Harrison's movements, and if he visits Ava, reporters are bound to find out, sooner or later. Once they do, any privacy we have will be over. I'd like to avoid a media circus as long as possible."

"I understand. I've lived in Harry's orbit for too long *not* to know how you feel."

"Thank you." She covered his hand with hers on the counter in an instinctive gesture.

He turned his hand palm up, threading his fingers through hers. "You're welcome."

She went still, her green eyes intent as she searched his face. "You're being very understanding about my concern, Justin."

He shrugged. "You're telling me you want the best for Ava and I feel the same."

"I hope so." Lily searched his face.

"You don't believe me?"

"I want to, I really do," she said slowly. "But trusting you isn't easy. I…cared for you, and I was totally unprepared to deal with how I felt when you left me." She saw his eyes darken, his body going taut and his fingers tightening on hers. She went on quickly before he could interrupt. "But I'm an adult and these things happen between men and women. This time it's Ava who'll get hurt if you suddenly decide to move on, and though she's very young, she's become attached to you. If you disappear from her life, she's going to miss you."

"I won't do that to her," Justin said. His voice rang with sincerity; his words were a vow. "I know you have reason not to believe me when I say it, but I swear, it's true. I'd never knowingly harm her, not in any way."

He cupped her cheek with his free hand. "I'll never knowingly harm you again, either. Never, Lily, I promise."

His thumb stroked over the arc of her cheekbone, calming her, the slow, repetitive strokes mesmerizing. Lily thought hazily that she should stop him, but she couldn't bring herself to protest when his mouth brushed hers. Once, twice, then his lips pressed hers. Warm, gentle, she felt as if the kiss somehow sealed his promise.

His cell phone rang, breaking the spell holding them with the efficiency of an alarm. Lily jerked away from him, smoothing a trembling hand over her hair.

"Lily..." His voice was rougher, deeper.

"You should answer that," she said, not wanting to talk about what had passed between them, not until she had time to think about it with a clear head.

He took the phone from his shirt pocket and flipped it open, frowning as he read the caller ID. "It's my assistant." He tucked the phone back into his pocket.

"Don't you need to take the call?" Lily eased away from him and then stood.

"I'll call him later." He rose and looked down at her, his face somber. "I need to know you believe me when I say I'm not walking away from you and Ava."

She stared at him, searching his face. "I want to believe you, Justin, but it's too soon. If you're still around, still making time for Ava a month from now, then maybe I'll start believing."

He winced. "I guess I deserve that." He drew a deep breath. "But, fair enough. Walk me to the door?" He held out his hand.

Lily hesitated, then took his hand, his warm palm callused beneath hers, his fingers closing around hers.

He stepped out onto the porch and looked down at her. "Tomorrow night? And I'll bring dinner— how about pizza from Zeke's?"

"I haven't had Zeke's pizza in ages—I'd love it."

"Good. Then I'll see you and Ava tomorrow."

He tugged her closer and kissed her, his mouth warm and persuasive against hers. When he released her, she could only stare at him. He smiled, a slow lift of his lips, closed his hands over her shoulders and nudged her inside, then pulled the door closed.

As Lily heard Justin drive away, she couldn't help hoping that this Justin, the man that seemed focused on Ava, would stay.

Chapter Six

Justin arrived with pizza just before five the following afternoon.

Lily breathed in the aroma, closing her eyes, and sighed. "I'd forgotten how good Zeke's pizza smells."

Justin grinned. "I'm hungry, how about you?"

"Starving," she answered promptly, determinedly ignoring the stutter of her heartbeat when his lips curved upward, his blue eyes laughing at her. "Let's go outside to eat—Ava and I set the table on the patio earlier."

Lily's town house had a small but well laid-out backyard. Six-foot-high board fences enclosed the area, lending privacy to the brick patio with its wicker umbrella table. Roses climbed the arch over the back gate leading out onto the alley, and one corner held a sandbox shaped like a turtle. A small swing set stood just beyond the sandbox.

"This is nice," Justin commented as he put the pizza box on the tabletop, glancing around. "Do you have a gardener?"

"No. I like taking care of the plants. I've discovered puttering in the garden is very therapeutic." Lily settled Ava into her high chair and poured a handful of oat cereal onto the tray.

"Can Ava eat pizza?" Justin asked, opening the box.

"No, she's too young for pizza."

Ava interrupted by banging her sippy cup on the metal tray and yelling loudly, pointing at the slice of pizza in Justin's hand.

"Are you sure?" he asked dubiously as the toddler babbled and waved her hand in demand.

"I'm sure." Lily laughed outright and sat, choosing the chair next to Ava. She toed off her pink flip-flops and wiggled her bare toes against the sun-warmed brick of the patio. The short cotton skirt of her sundress didn't quite reach her knees, and she spread a napkin over the bare tanned skin below the white hem. "You should see your face, Justin. Seriously, she may *want* pizza," she added when Ava continued to babble and wave at Justin. "But she can't have it."

"If you say so." Justin handed Lily a plate, frank male appreciation in his eyes as his gaze slowly moved from her face down to her toes, and leisurely back up again before he took a seat. "She's not happy about this."

"I know. She'll get over it," Lily assured him, determined to ignore the flare of heat that flushed her cheeks. "Lemonade?" He nodded and she lifted the pitcher, filling two glasses and passing one to him.

The wide canvas umbrella shaded them from

the late-afternoon sun. Bees buzzed in the pink hydrangeas along the back wall and the scents of lavender and roses filled the warm air.

Justin finished his pizza and stretched out his long legs, crossing his boots at the ankle to laze in the chair. "This is nice, Lily, really nice. How long have you lived here?"

"A little over a year. I moved in two months before Ava was born."

"How was that?" He asked, his voice curious.

"How was what—moving?"

"No, Ava being born…" His gaze switched to Ava, watching her little fingers chase the round cereal over the tray. "You weren't alone, were you?"

"No, I wasn't alone—Meggie was my birth coach and she was with me the whole time. And Aunt Shirley came to stay with me for the first two weeks when we came home from the hospital." Lily smiled at the memory. "I think the experience convinced Meggie she doesn't want to go through giving birth. She loves Ava and pretty much likes babies in general, but the process of being pregnant? Not so much."

"Was it bad?" Justin frowned. "How bad was it?"

"Just the usual—during the first three months I was nauseous the minute I woke up in the morning. I lost weight at first, and then, when I stopped losing my breakfast every day, I was hungry and craved the weirdest things. For some reason, I loved dill pickles dipped in peanut butter. The last couple of months I had a huge belly, couldn't bend over to tie my shoes, couldn't stand comfortably, couldn't sit comfortably, couldn't lie down comfortably...." Lily realized Justin's face had taken on a paler shade under his tan and his expression was frankly horrified. "Hey, it was a perfectly normal pregnancy."

"It doesn't sound like it," he muttered. "And if it was, I can't believe any woman ever has more than one kid."

"Nature blesses us by allowing the memory to fade," she assured him. "The specifics are already starting to blur for me and Ava's only a year old. I'm guessing by the time she's two years, I won't remember it as being so bad." She looked at Ava, smiling fondly.

"So you think you might like to have more children?"

Lily's gaze flew to his, aware the seemingly casual question was loaded with undercurrents. "I'm not sure," she said carefully. "Maybe. At the moment, Ava's all I can handle, and then some."

"Yeah, I can see how she could be." He looked away from her, studying the toddler's bowed head.

Ava looked up, saw him and immediately began to chatter, holding her arms out to him in an imperious gesture.

"I think she's ready to get down," Lily said.

Justin unhooked the high chair's seat belt with practiced ease and lifted the little girl, cuddling her for a moment before setting her on her feet next to Lily.

"Hi, punkin." Lily patted Ava's little hands where she clutched fistfuls of Lily's short skirt.

Ava chattered and bobbed up and down, then plunked down on the bricks.

"She had a mop of black curls when she was born," Lily said, smiling with affection at Ava as she crawled at high speed toward Justin. She reached him and pulled herself up, her hands grasping handfuls of his jeans. He grinned at her and leaned forward, swinging her up to perch comfortably on his lap. "Unlike lots of babies, she didn't lose any of it—it just got thicker and longer."

"Did you take pictures of her right after she was born?" he asked, brushing a kiss against the crown of Ava's head.

"Oh, yes, lots." Lily caught the wistful expression that flashed across his features. "I have photo albums, Justin. Would you like to look at them after Ava goes to bed?"

"Yeah," he said, his eyes warm. "I would."

Later, while Justin tucked Ava in, Lily took two thick albums of photos from the closet in her room and carried them downstairs.

"I don't know why I didn't think of these before," she told him as he joined her on the sofa. He didn't crowd her but the soft cushions of the sofa sank beneath his weight until her hip, thigh and knee nudged his. Her body came alive, hypersensitive to the heat and muscled hardness of him.

She flipped through several sleeves containing snapshots. "Here she is right after she was born."

He took the open album from her and laid it on his lap, tracing his fingertips over the first photo. "She's red and wrinkled—and look at how much dark hair she has. Plus, her face is all screwed-up and her mouth is wide open—was she screaming?"

"She definitely yelled," Lily said, laughing. "That little girl has a strong set of lungs."

"Which is good when you're just born, right?"

"Absolutely—it's a very good thing."

He flipped the page, scanning the photos and lingering on several pictures of Ava's tiny form, wrapped in a blanket and cuddled against Lily's chest.

"Don't look at those," Lily said quickly, leaning into him as she tried to turn the page. "I looked like death warmed over."

"You were beautiful." His gaze met hers and she stopped breathing at the emotion that blazed there. "How long did it take—the labor and birth?"

"I was in the hospital for almost eight hours before she was born."

He frowned, his dark brows drawing a vee above his eyes. "Is that normal?"

"Very," she assured him, seeing relief ease his expression. "I have friends who were in the hospital for an entire day or more."

A faint shudder twitched his shoulders. "I've helped cows, horses and dogs give birth. I can't imagine your being in labor for eight hours."

"It wasn't a lot of fun," Lily agreed, touched by his concern. "But look what I got when it was over." She pointed at a picture of Ava dressed in her going-home-from-hospital gown and bonnet.

"True." He studied the photo, a bemused smile curving his mouth. "She was so tiny," he muttered. "How much did she weigh?"

"Seven and a half pounds, which is a very good size, my doctor said." Lily felt the connection between Justin and herself strengthen, deepen as he lingered over the photos, asking her questions.

When Justin finally turned the last page, he closed the album and looked at Lily. "Thank you," he said softly.

"You're welcome. Would you like a copy of Ava's first-birthday picture?"

"Yeah, I would," he said. "But I wasn't talking about the photos." He leaned closer, gently splaying his hand over her midriff. "I meant thank you for having our baby. You could have terminated the pregnancy or given her away. I'm so damned grateful you chose not to."

The emotion in his voice brought tears to Lily's eyes. She covered his hand with hers, knowing her smile wobbled. "I'm glad, too. Finding out I was going to be a parent was scary, but even when the doctor was listing my options, I knew I wanted her."

"She's a lucky little girl," he murmured. "You're an amazing woman, Lily." He leaned into her, his hand a warm weight on her belly, and covered her mouth with his.

Lily sank into the kiss, allowing the heated demand of his lips on hers to pull her under.

She wrapped her arms around his neck, needing the feel of his warm skin and cool hair beneath her fingers.

His mouth left hers and he cupped her cheek,

tilting her face back to let his lips brush kisses down the arch of her throat. When he slipped the narrow straps of her dress off her shoulder and his mouth found first her collarbone, then the upper swell of her breast, Lily moaned and curled into him. Her breasts felt swollen and sensitive, the nipples peaking with a rush when his hand closed over her knee.

His fingers smoothed over her bare skin before slipping beneath her skirt to stroke higher, sending shivers of anticipation and arousal skittering over her nerves before they settled to pulse insistently, low in her abdomen.

"Justin," she murmured, knowing she had to stop him. Her voice was thready, aching with the desire to let him continue, knowing she'd regret this night if she gave in.

"Yes, baby?" he muttered, his thumb drawing circles on the sensitive skin of her inner thigh. "What is it?"

"I'm not ready, Justin," she managed to get out, shivering as he continued to stroke her with his thumb in small, testing circles. "I need more time." She closed her eyes and drew a deep breath, steadying herself.

She nearly wept with frustration when his hand left her thigh and he tugged her skirt lower, smoothing it carefully before his hand stilled, lying heavily against her knee.

"All right." Despite the tension in the hard chest muscles beneath her palms, he didn't try to persuade her. Instead, he brushed kisses against her mouth, lingering warm touches that almost had her groaning aloud.

Then he stood, pulling her up with him. "I've about used up my control for the night so I better leave. Walk me to the door?"

A half hour later, Lily lay awake, once again staring at the moonlight dancing across her bedroom ceiling.

Face it, she told herself, you're falling in love with him all over again.

She wasn't sure it would turn out any better than the last time. Loving Justin was complicated. She didn't doubt he cared deeply about Ava, and he certainly seemed to care about her, too. What she didn't know was if what he felt for her was solely because she was Ava's mother. Would he be so determined to stay in her life if they didn't share a daughter?

When she finally fell asleep sometime after midnight, Lily was no closer to solving the puzzle than was Justin.

The string of brass bells hanging on the shop door chimed softly. Lily glanced over her shoulder, expecting to see a customer, and found Justin. His broad shoulders stretched the black cotton of his T-shirt; the jeans he wore were snug and faded in all the right places.

"Good morning." Her smile widened, and for once she didn't bother trying to deny the quick lift of delight that filled her when she saw him.

"Hi." He ignored the three women shoppers eyeing him and paid no attention to Meggie as he dropped one arm over Lily's shoulder, pulled her close and pressed a swift, possessive kiss against her mouth.

Lily blinked as he let go of her, her brain scrambled by that quick meeting of mouths. "You're out early this morning," she said, concentrating on the words and telling herself to stop staring mindlessly at his mouth.

"I have to fly to Idaho," he told her. "The owner of a neighboring property I've been trying to buy for a year is finally ready to negotiate, but he insists on talking only to me."

Lily's elation disappeared but she kept the smile firmly fixed. "So you stopped by to say goodbye to Ava? I'll go get her—she's upstairs."

"No." He stopped her with a hand on her arm as she turned away. "I want you and Ava to come with me."

"To Idaho?" Lily blinked, startled and taken aback.

"Yeah, I might need to be there a few days and I thought you and Ava could see the ranch, check out the horses. I'm thinking we should get a pony for her when she's a little older."

"I don't think I can leave the shop...."

He stopped her with a forefinger across her lips. "Don't think, Lily. Just say you'll come."

"Yes," Meggie murmured beside her. "Go, already."

Lily glanced at her assistant to find her grinning and making shooing gestures. "But what about the shop? I just can't drop everything and leave."

"Of course you can," Meggie said firmly. "I'll look after the boutique. Sheila and Kate can take care of the orders upstairs and you can pack your drawing pencils and a pad of paper to take with you if you feel the need to work on new designs. Just go."

"Well…" Lily felt torn.

"What good is it to be the boss if you can't play hooky every now and then?" Justin put in, a smile in his voice as he coaxed.

"Well…" Lily hesitated. "I suppose we could be gone for a few days. But I have to be back by next Thursday for a meeting with a client," she added when he grinned at her. "Promise we'll be back by then?"

"Absolutely." He held up his hand, palm out, as if taking an oath. "I swear I'll have you back in time. We're using one of the company jets so even if I get hung up, which is unlikely, you and Ava can fly back whenever you're ready." Justin looked at his watch. "How soon can you be ready?"

Two hours later, Lily stepped out of the limo and onto the tarmac at Boeing Field.

"I'll take Ava," Justin told her, lifting her out of Lily's hold and settling her on his chest. "Hector, we'll need the car seat on the plane with us," he told the driver.

The chauffeur nodded and began to unload Lily's hastily packed suitcases from the open trunk. A second man in a flight uniform leaned inside the car and unstrapped Ava's seat.

"We can go aboard and settle in." Justin took Lily's elbow and they climbed the steps to the sleek jet. "Have you flown in a jet this size before?"

"No, only on commercial jets," she replied as they entered the cabin.

The interior was blue and gray with muted gold accents. It was tasteful and quietly luxurious; Lily liked it instantly. By the time they touched down on the private airstrip at Justin's ranch, she was in love with the comfortable plane.

"I'm totally spoiled. I'll never be happy flying commercial airlines again," she told Justin as the pilot taxied to a stop.

"It's nice, isn't it? Not to mention convenient." Justin gestured out the window on Lily's left. "Practically drops us off at my door."

The jet slowed and made a turn that allowed Lily to see a hangar. On the road just beyond, dust billowed up behind the wheels of an SUV and a pickup as they stopped next to what appeared to be an office door at one end of the large building. The drivers got out of their vehicles and joined a man in coveralls just outside.

"Do you always have a HuntCom plane available when you fly anywhere?" Lily asked as they waited for the jet to come to a full stop.

"Whenever I fly from Seattle to the ranch, yeah." Justin unlatched his seat belt and stood as the plane stopped moving. "If I fly farther, I sometimes fly commercial, but I try not to." He grinned at her, his dimples denting his cheeks.

"I can see why," she said, giving up trying to resist his charm and just enjoying the moment.

"One of the perks of being Harrison Hunt's son," he said dryly. "I'll get Ava."

While he freed the toddler's seat belt, Lily unhooked her own, and moments later they left the plane.

"Hey, boss," the oldest of the three cowboys called. "Good to see you. How was the trip?"

"Fine, Bob, good to be home." He drew Lily forward, his hand at her waist. "Lily, I'd like you to meet Bob Draper, he's my foreman and runs the place when I can't be here."

"Nice to meet you, ma'am." Bob touched the brim of his hat and nodded respectfully.

"Nice to meet you, Bob." Lily was charmed by the man's politeness and old-fashioned manners. The fingers that brushed his hat were gnarled with age and the hair beneath the brown Stetson was white. His bright blue eyes snapped with intelligence and interest.

"And this is our daughter, Ava." Justin's voice rang with pride.

"Well, now…" Bob fairly beamed. "It's a pleasure to meet you, little girl." He glanced at Lily, his wide grin including her. "She's as pretty as her mother."

"Thank you." Lily smiled back, intrigued by the obvious affection between Bob and Justin.

The other man in boots, jeans and cowboy hat approached, nodding gravely at Lily and smiling at Ava.

"We loaded the luggage in the pickup, boss, and put the baby car seat in the back of the SUV."

"Do you want me to drive you or should I head on up to the house with Cory?" Bob asked.

"I'll drive, thanks, Bob. I want to give Lily a short tour."

"Sure thing." Bob handed a set of keys to Justin. "I'll ride with Cory—and I'll let Agnes know you've landed and you're on your way."

"Don't tell her we've got company, Bob," Justin said with a smile at Lily. "I want to surprise her."

Bob laughed, a deep chuckle of amusement. "Oh, she'll be surprised, all right."

The two cowboys drove off in the pickup as

Lily walked beside Justin toward the other vehicle. "Who's Agnes?" She asked, wondering how many people were on the ranch.

"She's my housekeeper. I told you about her, remember? The woman I didn't want to lose so the boys and I cooked and kept house for ourselves at the old place I bought last year."

"Oh, yes," Lily nodded. "I remember."

"She's been with me for years," Justin said as they reached the SUV. He opened the front passenger door for Lily and handed her in before settling Ava in her seat and making sure she was securely belted. "I don't know what I'd do without her," he continued as he slid behind the wheel and switched on the engine. "Not that I'd tell her that," he smiled, with a curve of his lips that told Lily volumes about the affection he felt for the woman. "She already thinks she runs the place."

He put the vehicle in gear. The gravel road was well maintained and they followed it as it curved to the left to approach a cluster of outbuildings and barns. Lily could see the peak of a log house, but it wasn't until Justin passed a small grove of trees that she could see the entire home.

"Oh, my," she said, catching her breath. "What a beautiful house."

"I'm glad you think so. I like it." Justin's voice carried a deep thread of pride and pleasure.

The log home was two stories high at its center, with single-story wings off both sides. A deep porch ran the length of the entire front of the house, and rockers were spaced down its length, with two separate round wooden tables and chairs at each end.

Behind the house, a bluff rose, seeming to tower over the ranch and outbuildings as if sheltering the humans below.

"The center section is old," Justin told Lily as he parked in front of the house and they got out. "I added the south and north wings about ten years ago when I moved here."

"It's absolutely beautiful." Lily tipped her head back, scanning the facade of the building with its massive logs.

The screen door opened and two dogs barreled

out, barking ferociously as they raced down the steps.

"Boo, Rusty, down," Justin said with authority. The dogs instantly sat on their haunches, but their tails wagged their entire bodies and their eyes gleamed with excitement.

"I'm sorry, Justin. I didn't know you had someone with you or I wouldn't have let them out." The female voice was apologetic.

Lily looked up, away from the wildly excited dogs and at the porch. *Is this Agnes?*

The woman had to be at least six feet tall, she thought, and was dressed in a simple white cotton blouse over pale blue polyester pants. Her long feet were clad in Birkenstock sandals and her hair was cut short, in a curly bob that ended below her ears. Her face couldn't be called anything other than plain, but the lively blue eyes were filled with intelligence. And curiosity, Lily thought as she realized she was staring.

"It's all right, Agnes." Justin bent to run his palm over each of the dogs' heads, then lowered Ava so she could touch their soft fur. The larger of the two, a black-and-white collie mix, licked Ava's hand and she giggled, chattering to Justin. He laughed and shifted her higher, holding her securely. "You two, stay," he ordered. They complied, thought they clearly wanted to sniff Ava again and receive more attention.

"These two are cattle dogs, but I've made pets of them. They're in and out of the house," he explained to Lily as he settled his hand on her waist and urged her up the sidewalk to the porch.

"I think Ava likes them as much as they seem to like her," Lily commented.

"Smart dogs," Justin commented as they climbed the porch steps.

Agnes waited for them, her hands clasped in front of her, her face alive with curiosity.

"Agnes," Justin said, his eyes twinkling. "I'd like you to meet Lily Spencer and our daughter, Ava."

Agnes's eyes widened in shock and her hands flew to her mouth. "Your daughter?" Her eyes grew suspiciously damp. "Oh, my goodness. It's a pleasure to meet you, Lily."

"I'm glad to meet you, too, Agnes. Justin told me you're indispensable." Lily had the impression the older woman was going to enfold her in a spontaneous hug, but then Agnes appeared to catch herself and merely beamed at her before looking at Ava.

"She looks like you, Justin." Agnes's voice trembled.

"Yeah, she's got my hair and dimples, when she smiles." He tucked his chin, trying to see Ava's face. But she'd chosen that moment to be shy and was hiding her face against his neck. "Well—" he grinned at Agnes "—as soon as I can get her to laugh, you'll see the dimples." He drew in a deep breath. "What's for dinner? I'm starved."

"Oh, my." Agnes threw up her hands and pulled open the screen door. "I'm keeping you standing on the porch. Come in, come in. I had the boys take the suitcases upstairs." She gave Justin a reproving glance. "Wondered why you had so much luggage this trip."

"I wanted to surprise you. I asked Bob not to tell you I'd brought company."

"You surprised me, all right." She gave Ava a warm glance. "But it's a good surprise, a very good surprise." She took a tissue from her pants pocket and wiped her damp eyes. "If you'd like to show these ladies where they can wash up, I'll have dinner on the table by the time you come back downstairs."

"We won't be long," Justin assured her.

She nodded and hurried off.

"She's not what I expected," Lily commented as they climbed an open stairway that curved to the left of the entryway to a balcony above.

"No?" Justin looked down at her, a slight frown veeing his brows. "What did you expect?"

"I thought she was the woman you employed to care for your house. But she's more than that, she's like a beloved aunt, isn't she?"

Justin shrugged, his expression uncomfortable. "She's bossy, opinionated and thinks she runs the house and everyone in it. I suppose you could call Agnes more than an employee."

"Umm-hmm," Lily agreed. Justin may not want to admit he had a deep affection for the older woman, but he clearly did. And what was very nice is that Agnes seemed to feel the same for him.

They reached the top of the stairs and walked along the balcony.

"This is Ava's room." Justin pushed open a door.

Lily stepped over the threshold and stopped, gazing about her in surprise. "It's beautiful." As she registered the faint smell of fresh paint, she looked more closely at the beautiful white crib, changing table and dresser. "Justin, when did you have this done?"

"A few days after I found out about Ava."

She looked at him, searching his features but unable to decipher what this meant. "Were you so sure we'd come here with you?" she said carefully, trying to understand if the room was a reliable indication of Ava's permanence in his life.

"I wasn't sure at all." His gaze was intense, direct. "I hoped, Lily."

Something about the intensity of his words reassured her.

"I see. Well," she said softly, "it appears your hopes have been realized."

"Not all of them," he murmured, just as softly. "But two of them have come true today. Ava's here—and so are you."

"We're only visiting," she reminded him.

"I know." He gave her a lopsided grin and his dimples dented his cheeks.

"Stop being charming," she scolded, smiling back.

"Is it working?" he asked, his voice hopeful.

"I'm not telling." She glanced around the carpeted room. "I need to change Ava, but I don't see her bag."

"The boys probably dropped them all in my room. It's this way." He strode off down the hall and went inside the room at the far end. "Yeah, here they are. Which one is Ava's?"

Lily stopped on the threshold, her eyes widening as she took in the big room. The walls were white, except for two—one of which was all glass and looked out on the bluff, while the second one was a rock fireplace. A massive king-size bed sat against one wall and faced the fireplace, while an overstuffed chair and ottoman were placed to the right of the hearth.

A sudden mental image of herself and Justin making love on the big bed while a fire blazed in the fireplace caught her unawares. She stared wide-eyed at the turned-back sheets. When she finally managed to pull her gaze away from the technicolor visions heating her imagination, she saw the spa tub in the bathroom.

Lily nearly groaned aloud. Determinedly, she tore her gaze away from the temptation and stared at another wall. It was a moment before she could actually focus.

On the wall just inside the door were several framed photos in various sizes. All of them were of an elderly, white-haired man in boots, jeans and cowboy hat in various ranch settings with a young boy of eight or ten. Lily instantly recognized the boy by the black hair and dimples.

"Lily?" Justin looked over his shoulder at her. "What is it?"

"This room—it's—" she couldn't find a way to

tell him that she felt she'd glimpsed the real Justin here in the combination of simplicity and luxury, the solid furniture paired with the photos "—wonderful," she finished, unable to explain herself.

"Thanks." He swept the room with a quick glance. "The furniture was my grandfather's. I hired a decorator to plan the rest of the house but he didn't touch my room." He shrugged. "I didn't want him to—seemed fine the way it was, comfortable anyway."

"It's very nice," she said softly.

"Mama," Ava demanded, holding out her arms.

"Uh-oh, I think somebody's hungry," Lily said as she took the little girl from Justin. "Her things are in the red bag—if you'll bring it to her room, I'll get her changed and we can go downstairs and feed her."

"Us, too. I'm starving," Justin commented as he picked up the bag and followed Lily back to the nursery.

At eight-thirty that evening, Lily tucked an exhausted Ava into her crib, staying longer to make sure the little girl was truly asleep before tiptoe-ing out into the hall.

Justin was waiting for her at the bottom of the stairs.

"I thought she might not want to stay in a strange room, but I didn't hear her cry," he said as Lily reached him.

"She had an exciting day. She was so tired she fell asleep while I was rocking her and barely stirred when I settled her into the crib." Lily touched the sleeve of his shirt. "Are you going out?"

"We are, if you want to."

She glanced up the stairway, hesitating. "I can't leave Ava, Justin."

"Agnes will listen for her. I had the baby monitor in Ava's room wired into the kitchen, the laundry room, the living room, Agnes's room and the back patio. If Ava makes a sound, Agnes can hear her." He patted the breast pocket of his shirt. "And I have my cell phone so Agnes can reach us if she needs to."

"It certainly sounds as though you've covered all the bases," Lily conceded, touched and impressed by his concern and thoughtfulness. "Where are we going?"

"Not far. The nights turn chilly the minute the sun goes down. You'll need this." He draped a light denim jacket over her shoulders and took her hand, threading his fingers through hers.

Lily felt as if she placed more than her hand in his as he led her out of the house and down the steps to a four-wheel-drive pickup parked outside the gate. The sun was low on the western horizon, throwing long shadows behind them as they drove out of the ranchyard and followed the gravel road as it wound away from the headquarters.

The house and barns were quickly left behind as they began to climb.

"Where are we going?" she asked again.

"You'll see," he said, giving her a smile, his gaze warm on hers.

The grade of the road grew steeper and Lily braced herself against the dash as the road dipped and then climbed before ending in an open space on top of a high hill. The sun was a red ball, just easing below the horizon and far below them, the lights of the ranchhouse flicked on in the dusk. Lights came on in several of the other buildings, spilling pools of gold onto the porches.

"What a beautiful view," Lily murmured. "What's the long building just past the barn—the one with all the lighted windows?"

"The bunkhouse. Except for the foreman and the married couples, all the men who work for us live in the bunkhouse."

The truck windows were lowered and the faint sounds of a guitar drifted up to them.

"That's probably Cory," Justin said with a faint smile. "He's the musician among us."

"Was he with you at the older ranch you bought last year?" Lily asked, fascinated by this glimpse of the life Justin lived here on the ranch, so very different from the urban world of Seattle.

"Yeah, Cory was there. Besides playing the guitar, he's a pretty good cook." Justin caught her hand in his and tugged her across the seat, turning to lean his back against the door so she rested against his chest. "How do you like my ranch so far?"

"I like it," she said. Beneath her palm, his heart

beat in a strong, steady rhythm, the subtle scent of his aftershave mingling with the scent of trees and sage carried through the open windows by the night breeze. "Justin," she whispered when his finger brushed her hair behind her ear, returning to trail down her cheek. "I haven't parked with a guy since I was a teenager."

"I haven't kissed a girl in my pickup truck for at least that long, either," he said lazily. "I think it's time to try it again."

His mouth took hers, wooing her with slow, seductive pressure, and she gave in to his coaxing, sliding her arms around his neck, her fingers testing the silky warmth of his hair as she sank into the kiss.

Long, heated moments passed, and when he finally lifted his head, Lily was breathless. Her hair was rumpled and his hand stroked the bare skin of her midriff beneath the hem of her T-shirt.

"Now I remember why teenagers like trucks with bench seats," Justin murmured.

"Maybe we shouldn't have switched to bucket seats and sports cars after high school," Lily said, faintly breathless.

"I'm selling my car when I get back to Seattle and buying another pickup," Justin muttered, bending his head to trail his lips over her jawline. She tilted her head back, closing her eyes to better absorb the sheer pleasure of his warm mouth moving down her throat.

Beneath her silk T-shirt, his hand stroked higher, closing gently over the curve of her breast.

Lily stiffened and covered his hand with hers, the silk of her shirt separating his warm, hard hand from hers.

"Justin," she managed to get out, hardly recognizing the throaty voice as hers. "We have to stop."

"Why?" He nudged the scooped neckline of her T-shirt aside and kissed her shoulder.

"Because I'm not ready to go to bed with you."

He lifted his head, his fingers going still. For a long moment, his heavy-lidded eyes searched hers. "Are you sure? Because right now, honey, you sure as hell feel ready."

Her lips quirked as his thumb brushed over the peak of her breast. "Well, I'm not."

He lifted an eyebrow and tested the swollen tip of her breast with the pad of his thumb again.

"Parts of me may be more than ready, but the rest of me," she said with conviction, "is not."

He sighed and took his hand out from beneath her blouse, smoothing the silk back over her shoulder. "If you say so."

When she moved to push away from him, he trapped her hands against his chest. "You'll tell me, right? The minute all of you is ready to say 'yes'?"

"I will," she promised.

"Good." He pulled her back for a quick, hard kiss and then released her, easing upright as she moved back to her side of the seat. "Hey." He caught her, his hand closing over her forearm. "Don't go so far away, come back here." He tugged gently and she slid closer until she was tucked against him, her shoulder beneath his. "That's better."

He switched on the engine, twisting to rest his arm along the back of the seat and look out the rear window as he turned the truck around.

He drove with his right arm draped over Lily's shoulder, keeping her close as they drove down off the mountain and back to the ranch.

That evening created a shift in their relationship. Over the next few days, Lily slowly grew less wary of Justin and began to believe that perhaps the Justin she watched interacting with his ranch-hands and teasing Agnes was for real. In fact, she realized the Justin she'd seen since they'd arrived in Idaho was very much like the man she'd met in Seattle, before that dinner date when he'd inexplicably told her he was leaving her.

Chapter Seven

For the next few days, Justin devoted most of his time to Lily and Ava, although he spoke with his ranch foreman each morning and evening to discuss business.

Early one morning, Justin settled Ava on his shoulders and, with Lily, walked leisurely around the ranch buildings. They stopped in the barns so Ava could see the horses, which she had fallen in love with at first sight. Then they left the dim, fragrant barn for the bright sunlight.

"What's down there?" Lily asked, pointing at the dirt road that curved past the bunkhouse and disappeared around a small stand of trees.

"The foreman's house. There's a nice little spring just the other side of the trees and a small creek."

"Oh, Ava would love that! Can she wade in the water?"

"Sure. But it's cold, even at this time of year," he warned.

Despite wearing matching hats, both Lily and Ava's cheeks were flushed when they reached the shade of the trees.

"Whew." Lily fanned herself and reached up to test Ava's face with the back of her fingers. "You're warm, sweetie."

"August in Idaho gets hot," Justin agreed. "It's a little cooler under the trees."

The small spring bubbled out of the ground in the center of the small grove. Justin lowered Ava's feet into the water and she shrieked and kicked, spraying the adults. When she tired of the play, he hoisted her back onto his shoulders and she grasped handfuls of his hair.

They followed the creek through the grove and emerged on the other side.

"Who lives here?" Lily asked, pointed to a small two-story house with a neatly fenced yard.

"Bob Draper and his wife."

"It's nice," she said, noting the carefully tended plot of garden at the rear.

"I lived here when I was eight."

His words startled Lily. Justin was normally very reticent about his childhood. "It must have been a great place for a boy," she said carefully. "I bet you loved the woods."

He nodded, a slow smile curving his mouth. "In the winter, the creek would freeze and the deer and rabbits would leave tracks in the snow." He pointed at the second story. "My room was under the eaves upstairs. I could watch the deer on the bluff in back of the big house in the evening."

"You loved it here," Lily said, hearing the affection in his voice.

"Yeah, I did." His face grew somber. "My mother left me here when I was eight. Her father was the foreman. I'd never met my grandfather before and I wasn't expecting much after living with my mother. But he was a good man."

"How long did you live with him?"

"Four years. He caught pneumonia and passed away when I was twelve. His wife, my step-grandmother, wasn't well herself and since my mother was dead, she called Harry to come get me."

Lily caught her breath. "Your mother died?"

Justin shot her a quick glance. "She died of an overdose about a year after she left me here," he said without emotion.

"Oh, Justin." Lily had had no idea his early years had been so marred with tragedy.

"I didn't want to leave with Harry." Justin's lips quirked in a wry smile. He turned and pointed at the mountains that rose beyond the house and pastures, where white-faced Hereford cattle grazed. "I packed and headed for the hills, figuring I'd just wait him out and he'd leave, go back to the city. But Harry sent one of the ranchhands after me, and Gray came with him."

"Gray was here, too?" Lily asked, wanting him to keep talking.

"Yeah, and he told me Harry offered to buy this ranch and sell it back to me when I was grown, if I'd go live with him until I was older, had gone to school, et cetera. So I did—flew back to Seattle with them and stayed, but I spent summers here on the ranch. And as soon as I was out of college, I took over full time." He shrugged. "That's pretty much the story of my life."

"It's quite a story," Lily said softly. But not all of your life, she thought. He hadn't talked about the first eight years with his mother. She could only guess that those years hadn't been good.

She reached out and took his hand, threading her fingers through his, and they walked back through the woods to his home.

Later that afternoon, Lily and Ava joined Agnes in the kitchen. Ava happily played with her toys on the floor in the corner, safely away from stove and sink, while Lily helped Agnes prepare dinner.

"We took Ava to the creek by the foreman's house this morning," Lily said as she tore lettuce into a large teak salad bowl. "Justin said he used to live there with his grandfather when he was a little boy."

"Yes, that's when the Millers owned the ranch and his granddaddy was the foreman."

"Did you work here then?"

"Yes, I've been the housekeeper here for more than thirty years." Agnes laughed. "Don't look so surprised, I turned seventy-two on my last birthday."

"I never would have guessed," Lily said truthfully. "You look much younger."

"It's all this fresh country air and good living." The older woman winked at her. "Not to mention chocolate at least once a week."

"Ah, yes, chocolate," Lily agreed with a laugh.

"Did Justin say very much about living here with his grandfather?"

"He talked about how much he loved it here, watching the wildlife, the snow." Lily rinsed two large tomatoes and began to slice them. "He really loves it here, doesn't he."

"Yes, he does." Agnes paused, spoon in hand over the stove, and looked at Lily. "It's none of my business, I know, but I feel as if Justin's the son I never had, so I've got to ask—are you going to marry him this time?"

"This time?" The phrasing seemed odd to Lily and she glanced up. Agnes's expression was a mix of concern and determination.

"I'm only asking because I don't want to watch him go through any more pain. He nearly worked himself to death over the past couple of years and hardly ever smiled. When he showed up with you and Ava this week—well, it wasn't hard to figure out that the two of you must have split up about the time Justin stopped smiling." Agnes shook her head. "I've known that boy since he was eight and I've never seen him as happy as he's seemed with you and Ava."

Lily was stunned. Justin had grieved after he left her in Seattle?

"I didn't break up with Justin, Agnes, he broke up with me. I was head over heels in love with him."

"So what happened? Not that it's my business," Agnes hastened to add.

"I thought he didn't love me," Lily said slowly. "He said he thought we should date other people, hoped we'd remain friends—the usual lies a guy tells a woman when he's leaving her. To be honest,

I was in such shock when he told me I don't remember a lot of the rest of it."

"Oh, my." Agnes frowned in consternation. "I assumed you're the one who broke up with him. It never occurred to me that it could have been the other way around, especially not when I had to watch him every day. That boy was miserable."

Lily stared at the knife, forgotten in her hand, and the half-sliced tomato on the carving board. "But why did he leave unless he wanted to?"

"I have no idea. But after seeing the two of you together over the past few days, I hope you get it worked out this time around. I've never seen him so happy." Agnes eyed her keenly. "And unless I'm mistaken, you're still in love with him, aren't you…?"

Ava chose that moment to shriek, startling both women. She'd tangled her hair in the curves of a plastic rattle and was tugging on it but it wouldn't pull free.

Lily quickly wiped her hands and hurried to pick her up, untangling her hair and soothing her sobs. By the time the little girl was settled on the floor once again, the moment to answer Agnes's question was lost.

But Lily couldn't get their conversation out of her mind and continued to think about what Agnes had revealed about Justin.

Maybe there were deeper reasons why he'd broken up with her. But if there were, why hadn't he explained?

Chapter Eight

The comments from Agnes gave Lily new hope that she and Justin might have a future together. Determined though she was to have a frank conversation with him, however, there were several duties that demanded priority. Besides, she told herself, she wanted uninterrupted time with Justin, and that could happen only after Ava was tucked in and asleep for the night. She also needed to make her nightly call to her boutique manager in Seattle. So after she and Justin said good-night to

Ava, she told him she'd join him downstairs after making a few calls.

"Hi, boss." Meggie's familiar friendly voice was as clear as if she was in the next room instead of one state away. "How are our two city girls enjoying the country life?"

Lily laughed. "Just fine. The ranch is beautiful—the mountains, the horses, the cattle, the wildflowers." She paused to draw a breath. "And the house is gorgeous—it's built of huge logs and looks rustic on the outside, but the interior is positively luxurious. And the rooms feel homey and comfortable, despite the fabulous furnishings. You'd love it, Meggie, you really would."

"I'm looking forward to seeing it—you *are* going to invite me to visit you when you're living there, yes?" She teased.

"What makes you think I'm going to be living here?" Lily said mildly.

"I've seen the way your hunky cowboy looks at you," Meggie said with assurance. "Trust me, you're going to be living there. Justin's a man you should keep, and he looks more than willing."

I hope you're right, Lily thought. "How's everything at your end? Any problems with the shop?" she said aloud.

For the next few moments they discussed the highlights of Meggie's workday, the staff and the clients who'd dropped in at the boutique. Once again, Lily was reminded how very lucky she was to have an employee as efficient and reliable as Meggie.

After agreeing to check in the following evening, Meggie said good-night and Lily dropped the portable phone back into its charger. The house was quiet when she left her room and she paused to ease open the nursery door and slip inside. The glow from the night-light allowed her to see the crib and Ava, sleeping soundly on her back, arms flung wide, her black lashes making silky dark crescents against her downy skin.

Lily spread a light cotton blanket over the toddler, tucking it in at her waist, and left the room.

The plush carpet muffled her footsteps as she walked quietly down the hall toward the stairway.

The door to Justin's bedroom stood ajar and lamp-light inside threw a bar of gold into the hall. She thought she heard what sounded like a closet door sliding open and she paused, listening.

"Justin?" she called softly, knocking on the polished wood panel.

"Come in."

His voice was muffled, and when she stepped inside, she learned why. He stood with his back to her at the open closet. He wore only a pair of jeans, slung low on his hips, and the powerful muscles of his shoulders, biceps and bare back gleamed in the lamplight.

He glanced over his shoulder and saw her, a grin lighting his face. "Hey, did you reach Meggie?"

"Yes, everything's fine at the shop," Lily said, her throat going dry as she stared, unable to look away from the ripple and flex of powerful muscles. He slipped a cotton shirt off a hanger and shrugged into it as he turned to face her. The button-front shirt hung open down his chest, the blue cotton framing the strong column of his throat, powerful pecs, sleek washboard abs and the hair-roughened indentation of his navel. She had to struggle to remember what she'd meant to say. "And I just peeked in on Ava. She's sound asleep."

"Good." He walked toward her, his mouth curving in a smile that melted her bones. "That means we're alone, with the whole evening ahead of us and nothing to distract us."

He pushed the door closed and wrapped his arms around her waist from behind, dropping his head to nuzzle the sensitive skin of her neck, just below her ear.

She felt surrounded by him, his body strong, solid and protective at her back. She leaned into him and his arms tightened, pressing her closer. The temptation to turn and kiss him, to give in to the intimacy she craved, was strong, but Lily knew she couldn't until she had an answer to the question that plagued her. It was too important. "Justin, I talked with Agnes earlier today," she murmured, instinctively tilting her head to the side to give his lips better access. "I need to ask you a question, and I need an honest answer from you."

"Sure, honey." He kissed a trail down her throat to her shoulder, slipping the strap of her white cotton camisole top lower so his lips brushed her bare skin.

Lily shivered, licked her dry lips and swallowed, struggling to remember what she needed to ask him. "I thought you broke up with me in Seattle because you wanted to date other people and not me."

Their bodies were pressed together from head to thighs and Lily felt his big body tense.

"But Agnes told me you were visibly unhappy when you came back to the ranch," she continued. "And the time frame seemed to indicate you left me and almost immediately returned to Idaho."

"That's right," he admitted, his voice husky. "I left Seattle two days after I said goodbye at the restaurant."

Lily twisted in his arms to look up at him. "Then you didn't break up with me because you were tired of me?"

"No."

"Then tell me—why?"

"Is the reason really important?" he said, his eyes dark, his body strung with tension although his hands at her waist remained gentle.

"Yes." She caught his face between her palms. "I need to know what happened to us then. If I don't know why you left before, how can I trust it won't happen again?" When he remained silent, she tried again. "Was it another woman? Did you…?"

"No, hell no." His adamant denial was instant.

Relief flooded Lily. "Then tell me, please."

His eyes were bleak, dark with an emotion Lily couldn't identify.

"I thought I was doing the right thing by letting you go. You're the kind of woman a man marries—you deserve a man who's capable of being a good husband and father. I think I knew from the first that you wanted marriage and kids, but I couldn't leave you alone. The day before I said goodbye, we met for coffee at University Village, remember? There was a mother with a baby ahead of us in line at the coffee shop and you told me you'd like to have at least two children.

The truth hit me like a ton of bricks. I couldn't continue taking up your time, not when you should be free to connect with a man who could give you what you needed and deserved—a solid guy who would make a good husband.

"That wasn't me. Not even close. I knew it. I'd always known, but selfish son of a bitch that I am, I ignored it because I didn't want o give you up."

"You said goodbye because you didn't think you can be a good husband?" she asked in disbelief.

"Yeah, that's pretty much it." He thrust his fingers through his hair, rumpling it before he visibly braced himself for her response.

Lily stared into his eyes. She'd asked him for an honest answer, sincerity and conviction rang in his voice and shone from his eyes.

"That's the craziest thing I've every heard. And you actually believe it, don't you." She shook her head incredulously.

"I believe it because it's true. You have no idea what kind of life I've lived, Lily."

"I don't care if you lived on the street in Pioneer

Square and scavenged in Dumpsters or did time in juvenile hall," she said forcefully. "I care who you are now, and you're a good person, Justin."

His eyes narrowed over her. "You really believe that, don't you?"

"Yes," she said softly.

Relief eased the taut lines of his face. "I don't deserve you, Lily Spencer. But I want you and I swear I'll never make you sorry you gave me another chance," he vowed.

He lowered his head to brush soft, cherishing kisses over her cheeks, temples and the corners of her mouth. Lily slid her arms around his neck, threading her fingers into the soft thickness of his hair. When his lips covered hers at last, she moaned with relief. She didn't protest when he stripped the camisole from her and buried his face against the upper curve of her breast, his mouth hot against her already heated skin.

She didn't protest several moments later, either, when he bent and slipped an arm under her knees to pick her up.

He laid her on the bed without releasing her, his

body a welcome, warm weight that blanketed her. The edges of his unbuttoned shirt fell open, the powerful muscles of his chest softly abrading the swollen, sensitive tips of her breasts. He kissed her—hot, drugging kisses that had her moving restlessly beneath him.

His palm cupped her knee before his hand stroked up her thigh beneath the hem of her short shirt. She caught her breath when he brushed the back of his fingers against the damp, heated center that ached with wanting him.

"You're wearing too many clothes," he muttered, lifting his head.

She pushed his shirt off his shoulders and reached for the buttons of his jeans, their hands colliding as he stripped her skirt off over her hips and down her legs.

"Let me," he muttered, his voice dark and several tones deeper. He pushed off the bed and stood, shedding his shirt and jeans with swift efficiency. He took a foil packet from his jeans pocket, halting at the edge of the bed to stare down at her, his eyes hot.

Suddenly self-conscious, Lily's hands fluttered to cover her bare breasts and the pale pink thong she wore.

"No, don't," he demanded. "You're so damned beautiful, Lily. Don't hide from me."

He nudged her hands aside and bent over the bed, brushing hot, openmouthed kisses over each nipple before pressing his mouth against her navel.

Lily sucked in a breath, heat flooding her.

Justin tore open the foil, covered himself and slipped his fingers beneath the narrow straps riding on her hips to tug the pale panties down her legs. Then he gently pressed her knees apart and came down on top of her.

"Hurry," Lily murmured, frantic with the need to have him inside her.

He growled and took her mouth as his body claimed hers. Heat poured off him, increasing the inferno that burned her as they moved together. Lily shuddered with pleasure as the world exploded in lightning strikes and fireworks.

Lily woke in Justin's bed, his arm around her waist, anchoring her tightly against him.

"Good morning," his voice rumbled in her ear, husky with arousal.

"You're awake early," she murmured, smiling when he kissed her ear, his warm lips tickling. She wriggled, shifting against him, and a second later, found herself on her back, his warm weight pinning her to the bed.

"I never went to sleep." He brushed soft, tasting kisses across her cheek and throat.

"Not at all?" Surprised, she opened her eyes, scanning his rumpled hair, heavy-lidded eyes, and the day's growth of beard stubble darkening his cheeks and jawline.

"Nope. I didn't want to miss all those hours of holding you."

"Ooh, that's sweet." Her heart melted, her smile shaky.

His eyes darkened. "Not sweet, just practical," he grumbled. "We have to fly back to Seattle this morning." He nuzzled her cheek. "We should have wound up in this bed the first night we were here. Look how many nights we missed," he grumbled.

"Maybe we shouldn't waste these last few minutes?" she suggested hopefully, sliding her palm over the bare curve of his shoulder and down his back. The muscles flexed under her stroking hand, arching into her touch with obvious pleasure.

"Good plan," he growled just before his mouth took hers and his body blanketed her.

Chapter Nine

For the first time, Justin didn't mind leaving Idaho to fly to Seattle; Lily and Ava were with him. He dropped the two at Lily's town house and headed back downtown to his apartment. Contentment wasn't an emotion he was familiar with, he reflected, but it was the only word he could think of that came close to describing how he felt.

Making love with Lily the night before had been even more amazing than he'd remembered, and his memories had been pretty spectacular.

He still wasn't convinced he could break the workaholic instincts honed by years of living with Harry. He wanted to believe he'd always put Lily and Ava before work, but in a crisis, would he?

His cell phone rang and he glanced at the caller ID information; it was Harry.

"Alec Paxson wants you to join us to discuss final details tonight," Harry said without preamble.

Justin knew the man well. He'd been instrumental in negotiating HuntCom's purchase of Paxson's valuable real estate in downtown Seattle. He didn't question whether he needed to be at the meeting—the businessman routinely insisted on including him.

"Sure, what time?" Justin eased to a stop and prepared to wait. The Fremont Bridge was raised to let a tall-masted sailboat pass through and traffic was backed up on both sides of the lock.

"Eight o'clock. I reserved a table at the Save the Whales function—it's being held at the Collins Hotel. Why don't you bring Lily?" Harry added. "I bought a block of tickets and Cornelia will be there with Frankie. I'm sure they'd love to meet Lily."

"Right." Justin rolled his eyes. "Nice try, Harry. I'm not subjecting Lily to the Hunt clan until she decides she's ready. And dining with the Paxsons doesn't make me believe he's ready to finalize the deal and sign the contract. I'll pass on tonight. I'd rather spend time with Lily and Ava."

"What?" Harry sounded genuinely startled. "No, you have to be there—Paxson specifically asked for you."

"Sorry, Harry." Justin didn't feel a twinge of remorse at choosing his girls over a business meeting. "Unless you can convince me Paxson is really more interested in closing the deal than dancing with his wife—I won't be there."

"All right," Harry said with a touch of grumpiness. "Paxson wanted to hold the meeting at his office, but I convinced him to have the wives join us at the fund-raiser. I thought it would give us all an opportunity to get together outside the office for a change."

"You mean you hoped you could maneuver me into producing Lily so you could interrogate her," Justin said, convinced he was right.

"Maybe that was part of it," Harry admitted reluctantly.

"Probably closer to ninety-five percent," Justin said dryly.

"Regardless, Paxson wants you present at this last discussion before the contract is drawn up. HuntCom needs you there," Harry said firmly.

"All right," he said reluctantly. "I'll be there."

He thumbed his phone's Off button and dropped the receiver into the cup holder beside him. Ahead, the bridge slowly lowered and locked into place, then the traffic bars began to lift. While Justin waited for traffic to move once again, he drummed his fingertips on the steering wheel, turning over in his mind the possible complications caused by Harry's machinations.

He didn't want Lily to feel he was pressuring her to meet his family. She'd made it clear she wanted to preserve the illusion of being an average Seattle family of Mom, Dad and daughter for as long as they could. Tonight's event would be covered by local newspaper reporters and photographers. If he attended with Lily, photos of them together as a couple would be splashed all over the Pacific Northwest media by the following morning. The privacy they both cherished would be gone.

Much as he wanted to fast-forward his courtship to happily married status, he instinctively knew Lily needed time to accept and trust that this time they'd be together forever.

Which brought him back to the question of the meeting with Harry and Paxson. Was this one of those crisis moments he feared, and if so, should he go?

No, he decided. Both he and Lily had active careers. She'd probably be the first to tell him to meet with Harry and Paxson. So that only left the question of whether he should ask Lily to attend the dinner-dance cum business meeting with him.

He finally decided to tell her only the basic facts: Harry insisted he attend a meeting with a client. Period. End of story. No pressure on her to meet the family—no potential telling the world about their relationship.

He left his apartment early the following morning, made a quick stop at Starbucks for coffee and scones, and drove to Lily's town house.

She answered his knock fully dressed but with her hair tousled.

"Hi, what are you doing here? Did I forget plans?"

She looked endearingly confused and he grinned, kissed the tip of her nose, nudged her gently backward so he could close the door, then took her mouth in a kiss that left them both breathless.

"Wow," he said raggedly, when he let her go. "What a great way to start the day."

"Yes." She blinked up at him, bemused, a small smile playing on her lips.

"I brought coffee." He passed the steaming paper cup below her nose and she sighed blissfully, eyes half closing as she breathed in.

"Oh, yum. Whatever you want, you've got it."

"I'll remind you of that," he said huskily, watching her mouth as she drank.

She looked up at him from beneath her lashes. "Tonight?"

"I can't tonight," he said, following her into the kitchen where Ava immediately crowed with delight. "That's one of the reasons I'm here so early. Harry called—I have to join him for a meeting with a landowner tonight. I handled the negotiations and he wants me in on the final discussions before the contracts are drawn up." Justin unlatched Ava's seat belt and lifted her out of her high chair. She shrieked when he kissed her and made growling noises.

"We'll miss you," Lily told him, laughing when Ava grabbed fistfuls of Justin's hair and pulled.

"Ouch, you little demon," he complained, tugging her hands free. She babbled and patted his face in demand, so he repeated the bear growls.

"I brought scones," he told Lily when Ava finally tired of their game.

"I'll have to take mine to work with me," she said. "Look at the time. Yikes."

"You're the boss, can't you go in late this morning?"

"Not today." She disappeared into the bathroom off the front hall and reappeared moments later with her hair sleek and smooth. "I'm giving a new client a tour of the design room and shop at eight-thirty." She glanced at her watch. "And I have to scoot or I'll be late."

When Justin waved them off a brief ten minutes later and got into his own vehicle, he couldn't help but wish he didn't have to meet Harry tonight. He'd much rather spend the evening here with Lily and Ava.

Lily's plan to spend a quiet evening with just herself and Ava, minus Justin, ending with going to bed alone, changed drastically shortly after lunch.

"You forgot?" Sylvie Cross's voice rose in disbelief. "Hon, the Save the Whales fund-raiser is *the* event of the season. You have to go—you promised you'd wear the green dress, remember? Come on, Lily," she coaxed. "You can't let me down. I need the exposure. I need the clients and money you'll bring me by showing up in a Cross design. Pleeeease. I promise I'll return the favor in future."

"You'll be photographed in my lingerie at the Save the Whales fund-raiser next year?" Lily teased, amused as always by her friend's cajoling.

"Whoa, I'm not sure about that, but…maybe."

Lily burst out laughing, and after a few moments of listening to Sylvie catch her up on her latest boyfriend, followed by the latest juicy bit of gossip about a notorious Seattle model, she rang off.

Thinking her plans would definitely be different from the quiet night she'd planned, she dialed her neighbor and booked her to sit with Ava.

Lily chose to skip the dinner so she would be home to tuck Ava into bed before leaving the house. As a result, it was well after 10:00 p.m. before she arrived at the Collins Hotel and walked into the ladies' room, pausing in front of the full-length mirror. The emerald-green gown was one of her favorite creations from Sylvie, a gift after Lily had solved a crisis and volunteered to pair with the designer and provide lingerie at a local

fashion show. The event had been wildly successful and the designer became a devoted friend.

The strapless bodice was nearly backless and
snug as a bustier from the heart-shaped neckline
to just below her waist, where the skirt flared to
fall to her ankles. Panels of filmy green silk
covered the green satin skirt, and she wore green
backless strappy shoes with three-inch heels.

Lily tucked an errant curl back into the upswept
silky mass piled atop her head and secured with
an emerald-and-diamond clip.

"Excuse me, aren't you Lily Spencer?"

Lily hadn't noticed the tall blonde enter the
powder room. She was dressed in a stunning gown
of black lace, her brown eyes sparkling with lively
curiosity. Lily couldn't place the young woman
and was fairly certain they hadn't met before.

"Yes, I am." She smiled and held out her hand.
"And you are…?"

"Frankie Fairchild. I'm Cornelia Fairchild's
daughter—Justin's cousin. Well, we're not really
cousins, of course, but we always think of ourselves as cousins."

"How nice to meet you," Lily said with a smile. She'd known this day was inevitable—sooner or later, she was bound to run into family or friends of Justin's. She wondered how much Frankie knew about her and Justin.

"We're all just dying to meet you and Ava. I can't wait to tell my mother and sisters I met you tonight."

Apparently, Frankie knew the relevant details, Lily thought. "Justin's mentioned you and your mother," she said as she took one of the six dainty, velvet-upholstered stools at the long mirrored vanity table. "I'm looking forward to meeting her and your sisters. Your family is quite close to the Hunt family, isn't it?"

"Justin and I are good friends." Frankie took a seat beside Lily but didn't bother pretending to use the mirror. "I'm not so close to his brothers. You're just the sort of woman I thought Justin would pick," she said with blunt honesty.

"What type is that?" Lily asked, curious. She took out her lipstick and applied a fresh coat of peony pink.

"Gorgeous," Frankie said, laughing when Lily

lifted an eyebrow and eyed her in the mirror. "Well, you know what I mean. Justin only dates beautiful women. I bet Ava is the cutest baby ever—what with you and Justin for parents. Does she look more like you, or more like Justin?"

"She has Justin's dimples," Lily said with a smile. "And his black hair."

"I don't know why Justin didn't tell us you'd be here tonight. He must have wanted to surprise everyone—he didn't say a word about you earlier."

"Earlier?" Lily's hand froze on the gold lipstick case.

"At dinner," Frankie explained. "We all sat at the same table—Harry, Justin, mother, myself and the Paxsons." Frankie rolled her eyes and sighed. "Uncle Harry can't let any opportunity to close a deal go by. I swear, I heard Mr. Paxson promise Justin he'd drop by his office in the morning to sign the contract."

"I don't recall—what is it Mr. Paxson does?" Lily asked. Justin's business meeting was being held at a dinner-dance? Why hadn't he told her the meeting was a mix of business and pleasure, and more important, why hadn't he asked her to attend with him? Clearly, all women weren't excluded—only her. Her temper rose, flushing her cheeks.

"The Paxsons own two square blocks in north Seattle that Harry wants to buy. Justin handled the negotiations and Mr. Paxson wanted him present at the final meeting. He and his wife are nice—I think they're going to retire and travel more now. But enough about the Paxsons." Frankie waved her hand airily. "You and Justin are much more interesting."

Lily smiled and tucked her lipstick case into the small satin evening bag that matched her dress. "Well, Ava is, I'm sure."

"And you," Frankie assured her firmly. "When my mother told me about Harry threatening to disown the boys if they didn't marry, I thought it was the craziest thing I'd ever heard." She shook her head. "I was afraid Harry had suffered brain damage when he had the heart attack. But Justin and his brothers agreed and look how well it's turned out." She fairly beamed at Lily. "He's reunited with you and his little girl. And he's so obviously head over heels in love and happy—how romantic is that?"

"Indeed," Lily murmured, shock quickly evaporating beneath anger. She was so furious she actually considered screaming at the top of her lungs and throwing one of the dainty, upholstered stools through the mirror. *He lied to me,* she thought, feeling adrenaline pound through her veins. In the mirror, she saw a woman with flushed cheeks and green eyes bright with anger and hurt. "I've wondered why Justin agreed to cooperate with Harry," she said carefully. "It seems out of character for such an independent guy, don't you think?"

Frankie nodded. "I know, which is why I was astounded when my mother told me the boys had agreed to go along with Harry's scheme. But I'm sure Justin already knew he was in love with you. Besides—" she shook her head "—I'm not sure Justin wouldn't have cooperated even if he didn't have you and Ava. I understand Harry threatened to take away the ranch, and you know how Justin loves that place."

"Yes," Lily said. "I do know—he'd do anything to keep from losing it." She swung around on her stool and stood. "Let's join him, shall we?"

"Oh, yes." Clearly unaware she'd just spilled family secrets, Frankie smiled with delight and led the way to the ballroom.

They circled the crowded room, Lily following in Frankie's wake, since it was nearly impossible to walk two abreast in the throng.

"There they are." Frankie paused to point out a group standing near the French doors leading to the balcony.

Lily skipped over the two older women, a gray-haired man she didn't recognize, the taller, distinctive and unmistakable figure that was Harrison Hunt, and reached Justin.

He wore a classic black-and-white tuxedo with the same casual ease as the worn Levi's and shirt he'd worn at lunch earlier. Even in a crowd as well dressed and powerful as the one packing the ballroom, he stood out.

Her heart sped up, threatening to shatter the bubble of anger that shielded her from any feelings beyond outrage. For a brief moment, she was afraid the pain she knew was sure to arrive when the anger wore off would overwhelm her. But then she shored up her defenses, focused on Justin as they neared the group, and felt her anger surge.

She knew the instant he saw her. Surprise and pleasure brightened his face but were quickly replaced by concern. Before he could step toward her, however, she and Frankie reached the group.

"Hello, Justin, how lovely to see you…here." Before he could respond, Lily turned to Harry. "And how nice to see you *again,* Mr. Hunt." She looked pointedly at his thick mane of hair. "You left the Mariners hat at home this evening, I see."

"Lily," Justin began, his voice controlled.

"Don't worry, Justin, I don't plan to make a scene." She met his gaze with a level glance. "I just wanted to clarify a couple of things with your father." She turned back to Harry. "Is it true you threatened your sons to force them to marry and have children?"

Beside her, Justin cursed under his breath. Lily

held Harry's gaze, ignoring Justin and everyone else in the small group of elegantly clad people.

"There's a bit more to the story, but yes, that's the crux of our agreement," Harry agreed in a gruff voice.

"And did you also agree to modify the rules for Justin when you learned he already had a child?"

"Yes," he admitted.

"But the clause requiring him to marry the mother of his child or lose his ranch is still in effect, is that correct?"

"Yes."

Lily looked away from Harry at last to meet Justin's dark gaze. "Mr. Hunt," she said to Harry, her gaze still fixed on Justin. "I will never marry your son. Under no circumstances will my daughter and I be pawns in whatever game you're playing." She drew herself up, steeling her spine against the swift flash of pain that moved across Justin's features. Then his hard face became expressionless once again.

She swept the small group with a swift glance. The older couple, presumably the Paxsons, looked confused and intrigued. Frankie's and Cornelia's faces reflected shock and distress, although Lily thought she saw a glint of approval in the older woman's direct gaze. Harry, too, seemed pale beneath his tan.

"And you—" she glared at Harry "—should be ashamed of yourself. My daughter isn't another asset to add to your business holdings."

With that parting shot, she spun on her heel and left them, wending her way with determination, and sped through the crowded ballroom toward the exit. She snapped open her cell phone and called a cab.

Assured the driver would be waiting for her in front of the hotel, she rang off and dropped the phone back into her bag.

"Excuse me," she murmured once more as she tried to slip past a large group of people.

A hand closed over her upper arm. She knew without looking that it was Justin.

"Let go of me."

"We need to talk."

"No." She halted abruptly and turned. With

precise motions, she pulled her arm from his grip. "We don't."

His mouth tightened, a muscle flexing along his jawline, but he didn't protest when she spun toward the exit.

She knew he followed close on her heels, but she refused to acknowledge him.

"I know you're angry, Lily. You have a right to be. I can explain."

His voice was a deep rumble at her ear.

She didn't reply and kept walking.

She reached the long flight of marble steps that led to the lobby below.

He caught her elbow and gently but determinedly halted her on the landing, halfway to her destination.

"Lily, at least listen. Two minutes, that's all I ask."

She narrowed her eyes at him. "One," she shot back, glancing pointedly at the clock above the registration desk across the lobby below them.

"I apologize for not telling you my meeting wasn't in a corporate boardroom. But I didn't lie to you, tonight was all about business for me."

"I'm not finished with you because you didn't tell me you were coming here tonight, Justin," she said impatiently. "I'm furious with you because you lied to me about wanting me and Ava in your life."

"I didn't lie about wanting you, Lily. I'd want you even if there were no Ava and if Harry had never dreamed up his damned Bride Hunt." His voice was intense, his face reflecting the frustration he felt.

"You may be telling the truth," Lily told him, suddenly exhausted and on the verge of tears. "But I'll never know for sure, will I?"

He stared at her, his eyes bleak, his broad body tense.

"My cab's waiting. I have to go." She turned away, descended the marble steps and crossed the lobby to the exit. She didn't look back as she left the hotel.

She was in the cab, doors closed, before she allowed herself to cry.

Justin watched Lily as she moved across the lobby and through the exit without pausing or looking back.

This was the second time he'd had to watch her walk away from him, he thought grimly, and it was the last time.

He went back upstairs to look for Harry and found him in the nearly deserted hallway outside the ballroom.

"Cornelia and Frankie are still inside, saying good night to the Paxsons," Harry told him. "Our cars are being brought around to the front entrance." His keen gaze held remorse. "I'm sorry, son," he said, his normal brusqueness tempered with regret. "I never meant to cause trouble between you and Lily."

Justin's anger deflated like a pricked balloon. He dragged his fingers through his hair in an unconscious gesture of frustration. "I know you didn't, Harry. But the end result is the same, regardless of your good intentions. I'm going to do whatever it takes to convince Lily to marry me—which is why I'm dropping out of the Bride Hunt. You can do what you want with the ranch. I hope you won't penalize my brothers for my decision—in fact, I'm counting on your sense of fair play to waive the clause that requires all four of us to stay in the game until it's over."

"You'd give up the ranch for her?" Harry asked slowly, his keen eyes studying Justin.

"There are other ranches. And I'm wealthy in my own right, I'll buy another." Justin ignored the wrench of pain as he said the words. "But there's only one Lily."

A slow smile lit Harry's face. "Congratulations, son," he said, his voice husky with emotion. "You really love her, don't you."

It wasn't a question, but Justin responded, anyway. "Yeah, I really do."

"That's all I really wanted for my sons," Harry told him. "I didn't find a woman I could share my life with, despite trying four times. I think your Lily is a woman you can trust."

"Yeah, but can she trust me?" Justin muttered.

"What do you mean?"

"The men in this family are workaholics—we just naturally put business before family. What's the likelihood I won't let Lily down at some point?"

"Son, all married people let each other down at

some point. You apologize and try not to let it happen again. Not that I'm an expert on marriage, but I've heard Cornelia tell her girls that becoming a husband or wife doesn't mean you're perfect, it just means you keep trying to do your best, regardless of the circumstances. Besides," Harry grinned. "You put Lily and Ava before business just now—you gave up the ranch for them."

"Yeah, I guess I did."

"And because you did it for them," Harry went on, "I'm going to void your part of the contract and agree to let you bow out of the Bride Hunt without penalizing your brothers. I don't want them to know I've made an exception for you," he cautioned. "And I'll sell you the remaining acres of the ranch for current market value."

"No." Justin held up his hand and shook his head, adamant. "No, if Lily knows I benefited from this in any way, she'll always doubt my motives."

"All right." Harry nodded in agreement. "Then I'll give them to Ava on her next birthday."

"Harry—" Justin shook his head and gave in, a small smile of admiration curving his mouth

"—you're incorrigible. Do what you want with the land—just don't do anything with it that makes Lily distrust me any more than she already does."

"It's a deal." Harry held out his hand.

"Deal." Justin shook his father's hand and said good-night.

He drove home, making a mental list of all the things he needed to do tomorrow to set in motion the only plan he had left. He refused to consider it might not work, because he couldn't contemplate the alternative—losing Lily for good.

Thank God for Ava, Lily thought nearly once every hour over the next week. Caring for the toddler, together with a sudden rush of orders at the boutique, kept Lily busy during the days following her confrontation with Justin. The nights, however, were another story entirely. Despite working to the point of exhaustion, she couldn't seem to fall asleep, and even after she slept, Justin tormented her dreams. She woke in the morning feeling as weary as when she'd gone to bed.

She felt as if a part of herself had been torn away, her dreams shattered and her life as gray as the rainy Seattle sky. Despite the pain and grief that were her constant companions, however, she was determined to soldier her way through the days and not let Ava or her friends know her heart was broken. While Ava may have been fooled, Lily doubted she was as successful with Meggie.

To her surprise, Justin didn't call, nor did he appear at the shop. The Gazebo continued to deliver beautiful bouquets every three days, right on schedule, and she carried them next door to her neighbor, Mrs. Baker, who was delighted by them.

Exactly eight days after that fateful night at the Collins Hotel, Lily juggled Ava, her purse, keys and diaper bag and stepped out of her town house, heading for work. As she pulled the door closed and locked the dead bolt, she heard the door of the town house just beyond hers open.

"Good morning," she called over her shoulder, adjusting Ava on her hip as she turned, expecting to see the young couple who were her neighbors. Instead, a familiar tall, broad-shouldered, black-haired man with blue eyes stood on the porch. Just seeing him stole her breath and made her heart hurt.

"Good morning," Justin replied.

"Da-da! Da-da!" Ava burst into a long string of unintelligible chatter, punctuated by several repetitions of "Da-Da."

"Hi, punkin, how are you?" Justin's somber face lightened with a crooked grin.

"What are you doing here?" Lily asked, staring at first him, then the door to the town house.

"I live here now."

"But the Hargreaves live there." Lily couldn't get past the shock of seeing him in person when she'd been seeing him in her dreams all week. The reality was so much better.

"They used to. I bought the town house from them. They moved out two days ago and I moved in late last night."

"I didn't even know they were planning to sell."

"They weren't. I made them an offer they couldn't refuse," Justin said.

Lily stared at him, her brain finally beginning to resume its normal ability to function. "Why?" she asked, before the only possible answer hit her. "You're going to have me watched so you can sue me for custody, aren't you?" Unconsciously she tightened her grip on Ava.

Her words clearly startled Justin. "No, what makes you think that?"

She gestured at the town house. "Why else would you buy the town house next to me? No matter how many detectives you have following or watching me, you'll never prove I'm a bad mother."

"Lily," he said soothingly. "I'd never try to do that—besides, it wouldn't be possible. You're a wonderful mother to Ava—no court of law would ever say you weren't."

Her heart slowed its pounding. "Then why did you buy the town house? You have an apartment downtown."

"I bought it to be closer to you and Ava. I know you don't trust me, Lily, and I understand why. But as God is my witness, I don't want you because of Harry's ultimatum that all of his sons marry. I told him he can do what he likes with the ranch, I'm out of the Bride Hunt, as of last night."

Lily's traitorous heart leapt. Could it be true? Don't be a fool, the cynical side of her bruised heart replied, you can't trust him.

"I don't believe you," she said.

"I know you have cause to doubt me," he acknowledged. "Which is why I'm here. I'm staying for as long as it takes to prove you can trust me."

Lily could only stare at him, nonplussed. Maybe he *was* telling the truth.

"I have to go to work," she said finally.

"Then maybe I'll see you tonight," he responded. Without asking permission, he jogged down his steps and reached her in a few strides. He held out his hands for Ava, who nearly launched herself at him. He smiled, catching her and dropping a quick kiss on her cheek. "Can I carry the bag for you?"

"No, I've got it."

Moments later, Lily drove away from the curb, Ava securely belted into her car seat. Glancing in the rearview mirror, Lily saw Justin disappear back into his town house.

Unsure how she felt about this latest development, Lily spent her day trying not to think about Justin, and failing abysmally.

When her doorbell rang just before 6:00 p.m. that evening, she hesitated. She'd thought about this moment all day long. Should she let Justin in? Or should she ignore him? Reluctant though she was to allow him even a small foothold in her life, she knew they'd returned to square one and needed to work out a visitation schedule for Ava. And just as in the beginning, if they could reach an amicable decision between them before getting their attorneys involved, it would be better for Ava.

Besides, she had to admit Ava was overjoyed when she saw him this morning, she thought.

Scooping Ava off the floor, Lily carried her to the door with her.

"Hello." Justin's lazy smile made the single word a caress and a promise.

Lily refused to give in and smile back. "Come in."

"How was your day?" he asked, holding out his arms to Ava. As usual, the toddler nearly lurched out of Lily's hold.

"Fine." She gestured at the family room. "If you'll watch Ava, I need to put a load of her clothes in the washer."

"Sure. We'll play with the train."

Lily headed for the laundry room off the kitchen, glancing back to see Justin sit cross-legged on the floor, Ava balanced on his lap. He dragged the toy chest nearer and the two began to search through the wicker holder for the toddler-size Thomas the Tank train pieces.

When Lily returned with a basket of laundry to fold, Justin was stretched out on the floor, Ava sitting next to him, and both were deeply engrossed in pushing the trains in a circle. Ava mimicked the engine whistle sounds Justin tried to teach her.

Both adults purposely set aside deeper issues for the moment. But when Ava was tucked in bed at last, they returned downstairs to the family room, the air heavy with strain.

Lily leaned against the island counter and Justin remained standing as well, the kitchen cabinet counter at his back, his arms crossed over his chest.

"We should talk about visitation hours for you with Ava," Lily said.

"All right," he said slowly, his eyes darkening as he searched hers. "Have you thought about a schedule you can live with?"

"I've thought about the need for an arrangement," Lily admitted. "But I haven't come up with a plan that I believe will work for me. Have you thought of a schedule that's acceptable to you?"

"The only schedule that's ever going to be acceptable to me is to have us all living under the same roof, married to each other," Justin said bluntly.

"You know that's not going to happen," Lily said firmly, refusing to look away from his fierce eyes.

"Not yet." Justin pushed away from the counter and paced away several strides, hesitating before returning. "I know you don't want to hear anything approaching an apology or an explanation from me, Lily, but I'm asking you to listen. Please," he added.

She was torn. Should she listen to him again? Don't be a fool, whispered her cynical side.

"I want to tell you why I left two years ago. You were right, you need to know. Otherwise, you're not likely to trust me again." His voice was rough, filled with conviction.

"I'm too curious not to hear you out. But just because I'm listening doesn't mean I'll change my mind about us," she warned him.

"Understood." He returned to his former position, facing her across the narrow aisle between the island counter and the kitchen cabinets. "I don't know how much gossip you might have heard about my mother, but whatever you've heard," he said grimly, "it's probably true. She married Harry to trick him into getting her pregnant so she could sell the baby to him for a few million, which is pretty much what his first three wives had done. Somehow, her plan went wrong. When she told him she was pregnant, he didn't believe her. They had a huge fight and he threw her out.

"Within a month, she'd hooked up with another rich guy, and when I was born, she told him he was my father. She divorced him when I was two—I don't remember anything about him. I lived with her for the first eight years of my life. She hated my guts, but she kept me around and didn't tell Harry about me for revenge. She was alcohol- and drug-addicted for as long as I can remember. Her life was like a revolving door with men cycling through for a few months at a time before she moved on to the next one. The men were always rich."

Lily listened to Justin recite the details of his life with the same remote lack of interest as if he was reading from a stranger's case-history file. Even his eyes held no passion, no reaction at all to what must be painful memories.

"I told you I was eight years old when my mother dumped me with her father and step-mother. She never came back. I was ten when they told me she'd overdosed and died. I was twelve when my grandfather died and his wife called Harry. I swore on Grandad's grave that when I grew up, I'd live alone on the ranch in Idaho.

Harry bought it outright and told me he'd sell it to me when I was old enough to run it if I'd willingly live with him. You pretty much know the rest of it," he said. "I stayed with Harry in Seattle until I was out of college, then I went back to Idaho and the ranch. I own sixty percent of the ranch, Harry still holds forty percent. That's the acreage he threatened to sell off to a stranger if I didn't agree to marry and have children. I agreed, but only because Harry's health is questionable and because if I refused, my brothers would lose what they love most, too. And none of us did it for the money," he said, his eyes turning suddenly fierce. "None of us."

"But if you couldn't ask me to marry you two years ago, what's different now?" Lily asked, trying to remain neutral when she was outraged at the pain and neglect that she instinctively knew lay behind the bare-bones details of his childhood.

"I love you, Lily, but the only father-figure I know is Harry. He's a brilliant, single-minded shark, a workaholic, and he raised us to be the same. In fact, it never occurred to me to consider putting anything or anyone before business until I met you. I would have made your life hell, and sooner or later, I would have broken your heart and drove you away. All without knowing what I was doing wrong."

"Justin," Lily murmured, too shocked to speak above a whisper. "That's just not true. You're not like Harry at all, except for the intelligence."

"I hope you're right, Lily. Because I thought I could play Harry's game and arrange a marriage like a business deal, with a woman who cared as little for me as I did for her. But I couldn't start the process until I'd seen you one more time." He took one step and narrowed the distance between them to barely a foot. His hands took hers, cradling her palms in his. "And when I saw you, I knew I couldn't marry anyone else but you."

"I thought it was Ava you fell in love with that night," she whispered.

"I did fall in love with Ava," he admitted. "But she was the icing on the cake. It's you I can't live without."

"Are you sure?" Lily searched his face and found only stark honesty.

"Without a doubt." His grip on her hands tightened. "I have to warn you, though, I can't be sure I won't screw up and let you down at some point."

"I can't promise you I won't make mistakes, either, Justin. I doubt anyone can. We're only human. I won't expect you to be perfect one hundred percent of the time if you'll forgive me if I only make it seventy-five percent."

He stroked his fingers over the curve of her cheek. "Does this mean you'll forgive me?" he asked, his voice rasping with emotion.

"If you promise we can divide our time between Seattle and the ranch so I can keep my shop."

"As long as we share our life, I'm in."

"Me, too."

"Thank God," he muttered as he bent his head and took her mouth with his.

Lily went up on tiptoe and slipped her arms around his neck. She murmured in approval when he swept her up in his arms and climbed the stairs to her bedroom.

At last, she thought as he slipped her dress from her shoulders and trailed warm kisses down her throat.

"I love you," she murmured.

"Not nearly as much as I love you," he growled before he kissed her again and the world fell away.

Epilogue

December 5

Justin and Lily's wedding was the social event of Seattle's fall season. After the service at Bethany Presbyterian Church in Seattle's Queen Anne district, several hundred guests crowded the rooms of Harry's mansion for the reception.

"Is Ava with Cornelia?" Lily asked after nearly two hours of mingling and congratulations. She went up on tiptoe in an attempt to locate her daughter in the sea of chattering, laughing people.

Taller than her, Justin quickly located his aunt and their little girl. "Yes, they're talking with Harry and Gray," Justin assured her. His hand rested on her waist and he pulled her closer to whisper in her ear, "Have I told you how much I like your dress?" His fingers stroked slowly up her spine to her nape before returning to rest on her hip. "I'm looking forward to unbuttoning all these buttons later."

Lily felt her cheeks flush. She smoothed her palm over the soft satin of her skirt—floor-length and luxuriously full, with yards of beautiful fabric. Only the toes of her matching pumps peeped out from below the hem of the cream lace-and-satin wedding gown. The bodice's sweetheart neckline of cream satin was overlaid with lace that cupped her shoulders and threw patterned shadows over the upper swell of her breasts.

"I thought about that when I first saw the dress," she murmured, soft enough so only he would hear.

Justin's eyes darkened and he glanced at his watch. "How long before we can leave for the hotel?"

Lily laughed and patted his cheek. "We haven't even had the wedding toasts yet, and then we have to cut the cake."

"Let's speed this up." Justin took her hand and guided her through the crowd. Catching his brother J.T.'s attention, he mimed lifting a glass. J.T. grinned, nodded and spoke to a nearby waiter. Moments later, waitstaff moved thorough the crowded room, passing out filled champagne flutes.

Justin and Lily reached the group that included Cornelia, Ava, Harry, J.T. and Alex just as the waiters approached.

Lily sipped, the vintage champagne bubbly and tart against her tongue, as J.T. joined the nearby string quartet and claimed the microphone.

"Ladies and gentlemen, may I have your attention, please?"

The noise in the room lowered by several decibels and finally quieted completely, the crowd's attention fixed expectantly on J.T.

"I'd like to make a toast." He lifted his glass and turned to Justin and Lily. "To my little brother, who's found an amazing woman willing to marry him." The crowd laughed. J.T. grinned and winked at Lily. "Too bad she doesn't have three sisters just like her for the rest of us."

"I'll drink to that!" Harry lifted his glass.

Behind him, Gray and Alex exchanged wry glances.

"To Lily and Justin—may all your days be happy ones," J.T. declared, tilting his glass in salute before drinking.

It was another hour before Justin and Lily left the mansion. Ava was tucked in bed in the lavish nursery on the second floor, watched over by Cornelia and a delighted Harry.

As the limo pulled away from the mansion, headed for the Alexis Hotel for an overnight stay, Lily curled into Justin's arms.

"I thought this day would never get here," he murmured. "Have I told you how beautiful you are?"

"Yes, you did." She smiled. "But I never get tired of hearing it."

"God, I love you," he muttered against her throat.

"I love you, too, Justin. So much."

"You know I'm never letting you go," he said fiercely.

"Good," she whispered. "Because I never want you to."

* * * * *

The Bride Hunt continues!
Don't miss
THE MILLIONAIRE AND THE GLASS
SLIPPER
by Christine Flynn
The second book in the new
Special Edition Miniseries
THE HUNT FOR CINDERELLA
On sale December 20007,
wherever Silhouette Books are sold

SPECIAL EDITION

LIFE, LOVE AND FAMILY

*These contemporary romances will strike a chord
with you as heroines juggle life
and relationships on their way to true love.*
New York Times *bestselling author*
Linda Lael Miller
*brings you a BRAND-NEW contemporary story
featuring her fan-favorite McKettrick family.*

Meg McKettrick is surprised to be reunited
with her high school flame, Brad O'Ballivan.
After enjoying a career as a country-and-
western singer, Brad aches for a home and
family…and seeing Meg again makes him
realize he still loves her. But their pride
manages to interfere with love…until an
unexpected matchmaker gets involved.

*Turn the page for a sneak preview of
THE McKETTRICK WAY
by Linda Lael Miller
On sale November 20,
wherever books are sold.*

Brad shoved the truck into gear and drove to the bottom of the hill, where the road forked. Turn left, and he'd be home in five minutes. Turn right, and he was headed for Indian Rock.

He had no damn business going to Indian Rock.

He had nothing to say to Meg McKettrick, and if he never set eyes on the woman again, it would be two weeks too soon.

He turned right.

He couldn't have said why.

He just drove straight to the Dixie Dog Drive-In.

Back in the day, he and Meg used to meet at the Dixie Dog, by tacit agreement, when either of them had been away. It had been some kind of universe thing, purely intuitive.

Passing familiar landmarks, Brad told himself he ought to turn around. The old days were gone. Things had ended badly between him and Meg anyhow, and she wasn't going to be at the Dixie Dog.

He kept driving.

He rounded a bend, and there was the Dixie Dog. Its big neon sign, a giant hot dog, was all lit up and going through its corny sequence—first it was covered in red squiggles of light, meant to suggest ketchup, and then yellow, for mustard.

Brad pulled into one of the slots next to a speaker, rolled down the truck window and ordered.

A girl roller-skated out with the order about five minutes later.

When she wheeled up to the driver's window, smiling, her eyes went wide with recognition, and she dropped the tray with a clatter.

Silently Brad swore. Damn if he hadn't forgotten he was a famous country singer.

The girl, a skinny thing wearing too much eye makeup, immediately started to cry. "I'm sorry!" she sobbed, squatting to gather up the mess.

"It's okay," Brad answered quietly, leaning to look down at her, catching a glimpse of her plastic name tag. "It's okay, Mandy. No harm done."

"I'll get you another dog and a shake right away, Mr. O'Ballivan!"

"Mandy?"

She stared up at him pitifully, sniffling. Thanks to the copious tears, most of the goop on her eyes had slid south. "Yes?"

"When you go back inside, could you not mention seeing me?"

"But you're Brad O'Ballivan!"

"Yeah," he answered, suppressing a sigh. "I know."

She rolled a little closer. "You wouldn't happen to have a picture you could autograph for me, would you?"

"Not with me," Brad answered.

"You could sign this napkin, though," Mandy said. "It's only got a little chocolate on the corner."

Brad took the paper napkin and her order pen, and scrawled his name. Handed both items back through the window.

She turned and whizzed back toward the side entrance to the Dixie Dog.

Brad waited, marveling that he hadn't considered incidents like this one before he'd decided to come back home. In retrospect, it seemed shortsighted, to say the least, but the truth was, he'd expected to be—Brad O'Ballivan.

Presently Mandy skated back out again, and this time she managed to hold on to the tray.

"I didn't tell a soul!" she whispered. "But Heather and Darlene *both* asked me why my mascara was all smeared." Efficiently she hooked the tray onto the bottom edge of the window.

Brad extended payment, but Mandy shook her head.

"The boss said it's on the house, since I dumped your first order on the ground."

He smiled. "Okay, then. Thanks."

Mandy retreated, and Brad was just reaching for the food when a bright red Blazer whipped into the space beside his. The driver's door sprang open, crashing into the metal speaker, and somebody got out in a hurry.

Something quickened inside Brad.

And in the next moment Meg McKettrick was standing practically on his running board, her blue eyes blazing.

Brad grinned. "I guess you're not over me after all," he said.

SPECIAL EDITION™

brings you a heartwarming
new McKettrick's story from

NEW YORK TIMES BESTSELLING AUTHOR

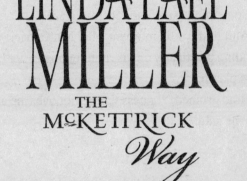

LINDA LAEL MILLER

THE McKETTRICK *Way*

Meg McKettrick is surprised to be reunited
with her high school flame, Brad O'Ballivan,
who has returned home to his family's
neighboring ranch. After seeing Meg again,
Brad realizes he still loves her. But the pride
of both manage to interfere with love...until
an unexpected matchmaker gets involved.

—— McKettrick Women ——

Available December wherever you buy books.

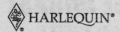

Kate Merrill had grown up convinced
that the most attractive men were incapable
of ever settling down. Yet the harder she
resisted the superstar photographer
Tyler Nichols, the more persistent the
handsome world traveler became.
So by the time Christmas arrived, there
was only one wish on her holiday list—
that she was wrong!

LOOK FOR

THE CHRISTMAS DATE

BY

Michele Dunaway

**Available December
wherever you buy books**

REQUEST YOUR FREE BOOKS!

2 FREE NOVELS PLUS 2 FREE GIFTS!

SPECIAL EDITION®

Life, Love and Family!

YES! Please send me 2 FREE Silhouette Special Edition® novels and my 2 FREE gifts. After receiving them, if I don't wish to receive any more books, I can return the shipping statement marked "cancel." If I don't cancel, I will receive 6 brand-new novels every month and be billed just $4.24 per book in the U.S., or $4.99 per book in Canada, plus 25¢ shipping and handling per book and applicable taxes, if any*. That's a savings of at least 15% off the cover price! I understand that accepting the 2 free books and gifts places me under no obligation to buy anything. I can always return a shipment and cancel at any time. Even if I never buy another book from Silhouette, the two free books and gifts are mine to keep forever.   235 SDN EEYU 335 SDN EEY6

Name   (PLEASE PRINT)

Address   Apt.

City   State/Prov.   Zip/Postal Code

Signature (if under 18, a parent or guardian must sign)

Mail to the **Silhouette Reader Service™:**
IN U.S.A.: P.O. Box 1867, Buffalo, NY 14240-1867
IN CANADA: P.O. Box 609, Fort Erie, Ontario L2A 5X3

Not valid to current Silhouette Special Edition subscribers.

Want to try two free books from another line?
Call 1-800-873-8635 or visit www.morefreebooks.com.

* Terms and prices subject to change without notice. NY residents add applicable sales tax. Canadian residents will be charged applicable provincial taxes and GST. This offer is limited to one order per household. All orders subject to approval. Credit or debit balances in a customer's account(s) may be offset by any other outstanding balance owed by or to the customer. Please allow 4 to 6 weeks for delivery.

Your Privacy: Silhouette is committed to protecting your privacy. Our Privacy Policy is available online at www.eHarlequin.com or upon request from the Reader Service. From time to time we make our lists of customers available to reputable firms who may have a product or service of interest to you. If you would prefer we not share your name and address, please check here. ☐

Get ready to meet

THREE WISE WOMEN

with stories by

DONNA BIRDSELL,
LISA CHILDS

and

SUSAN CROSBY.

Don't miss these three unforgettable stories
about modern-day women and the love
and new lives they find on Christmas.

Look for *Three Wise Women*
Available December wherever you buy books.

TheNextNovel.com

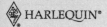

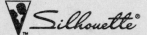

COMING NEXT MONTH

#1867 THE McKETTRICK WAY—Linda Lael Miller
Meg McKettrick longed for a baby—husband optional—and her
rugged old flame, rodeo cowboy Brad O'Ballivan, was perfect father
material. But Brad didn't want a single night of passion, he wanted
love, marriage, the works. Now it was an epic battle of wills, as proud,
stubborn Meg insisted on doing things her way…the McKettrick way.

#1868 A BRAVO CHRISTMAS REUNION—Christine Rimmer
Bravo Family Ties
Try as he might, coffeehouse-chain tycoon Marcus Reid couldn't get
over his former executive assistant Hayley Bravo. But when Hayley
had proposed to him seven months ago, he'd balked and she'd left
town. Now a business trip reunited them…and clued Marcus in to the
real reason for Hayley's proposal—he was about to be a daddy!

#1869 A COWBOY UNDER HER TREE—Allison Leigh
Montana Mavericks: Striking It Rich
Hotel heiress Melanie McFarlane took over Thunder Canyon Ranch to
prove she could run a successful business on her own. But she needed
help—bad—and enlisted local rancher Russ Chilton, telling her family
he was her husband. Russ insisted on a legal marriage to seal the deal,
and soon city slicker Melanie fell hard…for her husband.

#1870 THE MILLIONAIRE AND THE GLASS SLIPPER—
Christine Flynn
The Hunt for Cinderella
When his tech mogul father delivered the ultimatum to marry and
have kids within a year or be disinherited, family rebel J. T. Hunt
decided to set up his own business before he was cut off. For help, he
turned to a bubbly blond ad exec—but it was her subtly beautiful stepsister,
Amy Kelton, who rode to the rescue as J.T.'s very own Cinderella.

#1871 HER CHRISTMAS SURPRISE—Kristin Hardy
Kelly Stafford thought she was engaged to the *good* Alexander
sibling—until she walked in on him with another woman, and his
money laundering threatened to land Kelly in jail! Now could his
black-sheep brother, Lex Alexander—voted Most Likely To Get
Arrested back in high school—save Kelly…and maybe even steal
her heart in the process?

#1872 THE TYCOON MEETS HIS MATCH—
Barbara Benedict
Sure it was surprising when writer Trae Andrelini's independent friend
Lucy decided to marry stuffed-shirted mogul Rhys Paxton for security,
and even more surprising when Lucy left him at the altar to go after an
old boyfriend. But the biggest surprise of all? When free-spirited Trae
discovered that Rhys was actually the man for *her!*

SSECNM1107